Shattered

Broken Trilogy, Book Two

J.L.Drake

Shattered

Copyright © 2015 by J.L. Drake.
All rights reserved.
First Print Edition: May 2015

Limitless Publishing, LLC
Kailua, HI 96734
www.limitlesspublishing.com

Formatting: Limitless Publishing

ISBN-13: 978-1-64034-915-5

No part of this book may be reproduced, scanned, or distributed in any printed or electronic form without permission. Please do not participate in or encourage piracy of copyrighted materials in violation of the author's rights. Thank you for respecting the hard work of this author.

This is a work of fiction. Names, characters, places, and incidents either are the product of the author's imagination or are used fictitiously, and any resemblance to locales, events, business establishments, or actual persons—living or dead—is entirely coincidental.

Dedication

Mom,
Once shattered, we came out stronger.
The internal scars remind us,
that life is precious and fragile.
Thank you for being our mother,
our rock, and our best friend.

Prologue

There's a difference between living and surviving, and this was neither. My life was never going forward. It had always been on hold while I dealt with everyone else—my mother, my father, my keepers. I was finally gifted a few months in which I fell in love with a man who made me feel more alive than I ever thought possible. Now, because of me, he's been ripped from my life, murdered in the worst way possible for all of us to witness, and I lost our unplanned baby. There is nothing of me left to pick up the pieces; I don't even want to. So here I am, gun to my head, waiting to join my little family on the other side.

Chapter One

Somewhere in México

Cole

"You did what, Raul?" The American hisses at the man who wears the ridiculous longhorn belt buckle.

"No-no, *señor*, he's alive, see?" He steps out of The American's view to show that, yes, Cole is indeed alive. "No harm done."

"No harm?" The American pulls out a knife, grabs Raul's hand, slams it against the wall, and within a blink the man's pointer finger is rolling on the floor.

"Ahhh!" Raul yells.

"He's our only leverage! And now they think he's dead. Fuck!" The American punches the blood-splattered wall. He turns to face Raul, whose white face is staring at his missing digit. "If you weren't married to my cousin, I swear I'd behead you myself."

"*Sí*," the man responds weakly.

Luka wipes his mouth with a rag. The smell of blood must be getting to him. He glances at Cole, who's watching them. The corners of his mouth tug upward. He likes seeing Luka's weaknesses.

***

Savannah

I stare forward, hands shaking, tears streaming down my face. I'm so close to them. If only...

The ring of Keith's phone rips through the silence, making my finger freeze, trembling on the trigger. I squeeze my eyes shut and try to focus.

"What?" Keith's raspy voice answers. "Wait, back up. What?" My eyes slowly open, and I see Keith's head turn toward me. His face falls as he notices what's in my hand. "Wait!" He drops his phone, and it bounces off the floor as he jumps to his feet. "Savannah?"

"Stop," I cry, shaking my head and keeping the gun tight to my temple. He stops at the end of the bed, his hands raised to show he won't move.

"Please, Savi, give me the gun. Mark just called with—"

"Stop," I cry out again through a sob. I'm so close. "Just leave me."

"No." He doesn't elaborate.

"I don't want to hurt anymore. I have so much pain. I don't want to live without him. I don't want to live without our baby." I drop my head and pull up my knees. Keith can see I'm moments from ending it all. *Just squeeze the trigger, Savannah!* I keep a firm grip on the gun that's imprinting my temple. "At what point did fate decide I don't deserve to be happy?" I scream as memories pour out of me. "I've served my time. I watched my mother die. I watched my father pull away and stop loving me. I was kidnapped, and I had a birthday trapped in a twenty-four by twenty-four room! Now I lose my lover and our baby! I don't want to know what's next, Keith—I just can't!" The gun bounces around on my head as my sobs become louder. "Everyone I love leaves me. I just want it to end!"

"I know, Savannah." He kneels on the bed and shifts toward me. "But this is isn't the way." He moves up next to me and runs a steady, slow hand up my arm and over my hand. Wrapping his fingers around mine, he whispers, "Give it to me, sweetheart, please."

Suddenly the weight of my pain is too much. It makes my hand relax enough that he slips the gun from my grip. He grabs my shoulders and pulls me into him. I feel him start to shake.

"I miss him too," he barely whispers.

This is my undoing; I completely break down.

I am a coward.

***

Mark

Mark races up the stairs and down the long hallway toward Cole's room. He flies into the bedroom and sees Savannah, curled up in a ball sobbing, and Keith looking terrified.

"What? What's going on?"

Keith shakes his head as he holds up the gun. Mark feels the blood rush from his face when he realizes what could have happened. He grips his hair as he tries to think clearly. He needs to speak with Keith and Daniel *now*.

"Keith," he says quietly, feeling ill, "Cole's office, five minutes." Keith nods.

He turns and runs out of the room and into Abigail's, which she has been sharing with her sister June.

"Abby!" Mark hisses as he snaps on the light. "I need your help."

"Huh?" June squints at the sudden brightness.

Abigail reaches for her robe. "Mark, dear, what's wrong?"

"I need…" He pauses to control to his jumbled thoughts. "Where's Sue?"

"With Savannah. Why?"

Mark shakes his head. "I need you to go in Cole's room and wait with Savi. Something happened, and I don't want her to be alone. I—"

Abigail pulls on her slippers. "What happened? Where's Keith?"

"I need a meeting. I-I think I found something." He starts to leave, but turns. "Abby, you know better than anyone where Cole might have weapons stashed around his room. Please get rid of them."

She looks at June, baffled, then nods at Mark.

Mark bangs on the spare bedroom door, yelling out Daniel's name. Sue answers first, looking exhausted.

"Sue! You need to go see Savi." Her face drops

as she pushes by him and runs down the hall. Mark moves into the room and sees Daniel pulling on a T-shirt. "I need to speak with you now." Shrieks from Cole's room make Mark squeeze his eyes shut.

Holy shit, this is out of control.

***

Mark is busy pulling up the file, while everyone plays catch-up.

"Jesus Christ!" Daniel rubs his head, listening to Keith's story.

"If Mark hadn't called…" Keith's hands drop heavily to his sides. "I-I thought she was all right. She's been so quiet, I thought she was dealing with all this in her own way. I had no idea she'd go this far."

"Guys," Mark interrupts, pointing to the flat screen, "tell me what you see." He presses play on the DVD from The American. Daniel shoots Mark a nasty look. "I know, believe me, I know, but just watch, please."

Daniel takes a deep breath and watches his son's murder all over again, but this time he steps a little closer.

"Wait," Mark says, and Keith moves next to Daniel.

"Oh my god!" Daniel's head jerks toward Mark. "There's no tattoo!"

"Exactly." Mark nods, freezing the video with the man's shoulder in view. "That man isn't Cole."

Daniel picks up the phone and makes a quick call before returning to the stunned group. "Frank will be here in an hour. Get the guys up. We need to have a meeting."

"What do you think we should do?" Keith asks.

Daniel folds his arms. "Get the guys prepared. We move out tonight."

"I'm coming." Mark's tone is stern as he removes his sling.

"Yeah, you are." Daniel nods and looks at John. "Paul can't come. Have Derek take his place."

Mark stops mid-step, hating how much his team despises Derek. "Not Keith or Mike?"

Daniel turns to Keith. "Savannah or Cole?"

Keith runs his hand over his forehead. Mark knows he's close with Savannah, and she trusts him more than anyone in the house, but the idea of bringing back Cole is tempting. "Cole."

"Okay," Daniel agrees. "Living room meeting at zero two hundred hours."

Half an hour later Mark waits while zoned out, trying to sort his thoughts and mentally prepare for what's to come. What if they're too late? What if Cole tried to escape after that video and they had to kill him? Mike sits bouncing his knee and watching Mark pace the living room. Derek sits next to Mike, half asleep. He yawns loudly, making Mike glare at him.

"Show some respect, Derek."

"I was out cold, Mike. It's just a natural reaction when one gets awakened the way John woke me."

"Stop talking—"

"Guys," Mark whispers, shaking his head. Now is not the time for a pissing match. Emotions are too high.

John walks behind Paul, who is limping along on a crutch from his recent knife wound to the leg. Daniel appears with his wife, Sue. He sits her down on a chair. She looks confused but keeps glancing back at the stairs. No doubt she would rather be with Savannah than here with everyone else.

"I'm here," Frank announces, bursting through the front door. He doesn't bother taking his boots off as he sits down on the couch.

"All right," Daniel addresses the room. "I'm making this short and sweet. The man who was killed on that tape wasn't Cole." The room is so quiet you'd think someone pressed a pause button. "When the body twists in the video, the man doesn't have a tattoo on his shoulder, and we all know Cole has his Special Forces one."

"Yeah, that's right," Paul chimes in. "So—"

"How confident are you it's not him?" Frank moves his attention over to Daniel.

"I've watched it two more times, and I'm one hundred percent confident the man on that tape is not my son."

Frank stands and pulls out his cell phone. "Good enough for me. Give me a minute." He heads for the kitchen.

"Dan?" Sue whispers from her chair. "I don't think we should say anything to Savannah until we know what we're dealing with. I don't think she can handle it." A tear slips down her cheek, and Mark's stomach twists tighter. "I don't think I could handle seeing her shatter the last piece that's holding her together."

Daniel walks across the room, taking his wife's

hand in his. "I agree, dear."

"You will go too." She stands stiffly, wrapping her sweater around her hunched body. She looks like she's barely holding on to her emotions.

"Yes."

She nods. "Go bring our son home." He reaches over and gives her a kiss on the cheek, then watches her move toward the stairs, the shock of the evening's events making her move like a zombie. Daniel sighs then turns to look at everyone just as Frank returns.

"All right, we have a possible location. We have two scouts watching the house. It's in a small town right outside Tijuana."

Dan steps forward, wiping his sweaty palms across his weathered face. "Since Paul is out, Keith will take his place and Mike will be in charge of the house." Derek begins to argue, but Daniel shakes his head, stopping him. "The team needs absolute trust, Derek. You've shown that you don't work well in a unit. Until you prove yourself, you're staying here." Derek leans back, muttering under his breath.

"I'll give you access to anything you need," Frank informs them. "I need this to be a quick extraction. Get him out of there before we start an even bigger goddamn war with those assholes, though I'm not opposed to lighting the whole place up on your way out." Frank rubs his face roughly. "Chopper will be here in thirty."

"Okay, men, let's move it," Daniel orders as everyone quickly scatters. "Frank, I need to see the blueprints for the house."

Abigail clears her throat. "What if—"

"No," Daniel whispers, looking grim, "no what if's."

She nods and gives Mark a quick hug. "Be careful, my boy." She kisses his cheek. "We're having prime rib."

Mark grins a little. "Well, in that case…" He stops himself as the painful lump rises.

"I know, sweetie." She runs her hand along his cheek. "He's going to be okay."

"Yeah," he sighs, hoping to anyone who is listening to make his best friend be alive.

***

Savannah

I sit in Cole's tub and stare out the window. I can hear June and Sue whispering about something when Abigail comes into the bathroom. She shuts the door, then comes to sit in the leather chair across from me. It's two in the morning, and since my pathetic attempt at suicide failed I have everyone in the house awake.

"Are we going to have to put you in a padded room, Savi?" she asks, making my heart squeeze. "I know you're hurting; we all are, but don't bring more hurt to this family by ending your life." I pull my knees up to my chest and wrap my arms around them. She sighs then clears her throat. "I'm so sorry, Savannah, about the baby."

"Please," I swallow around a sob lodged in my throat, "don't."

She moves behind me and starts pouring warm water over my hair. We don't speak again as she washes my hair, dries me off, and then walks me down to the kitchen. I'm very aware of the atmosphere in the house, and I'm sure it's due to what I have done. The level of anxiety is like an elephant in the room.

We pass a couple of guys who quickly stop talking as we approach. They don't look at me. Daniel comes into the room looking like he's on a mission. I look away, but he wraps his arms around my shoulders, pulling me into him much like his son used to do. I fight like hell to stop my tears, but it's no use. They are always ready to break the dam that is made of frigging toothpicks.

"Some of us have been called out for an assignment," he says, pulling away to look at me. "Mike is in charge since Keith is filling in for Paul." He looks over at Abigail. "We shouldn't be any longer than forty-eight hours." He steps back and walks out of the room. I want to ask why he's going, but I concentrate on trying to stop my annoying crying instead. I cried like crazy over my mother's death, but this is a different kind of loss. My heart is shattered forever, and I know that even though I did not end my life today I have no desire to go on.

"Savannah," Keith says as he slips onto the stool next to me, "will you be all right while I'm gone?" I nod, feeling very tired. He takes my chin in his hand "Savi, Mike is easy to talk to, and Derek will be hovering around more than normal. None of your disappearing acts, you hear me? Right now with

The American—"

"I won't," I cut him off, pushing up from my stool. "Be safe," I whisper as I walk out into the living room and sit down in my favorite place in front of the fire. Scoot, the little shit housecat, comes immediately to me and rolls onto his back, flops his legs open, and purrs until I give him some attention. I let my mind wander, remembering sitting on the floor scratching Scoot when Cole first joined me. Cole rubbed his belly with the warmest smile. I wipe my cheeks. Lowering my head to the floor, I tune in to the crackle of the fire.

"Merry Christmas," I whisper as I kiss Scoot's furry head and slowly drift off to sleep.

***

Cole

Cole presses his mouth to the small hole in the wall, attempting to suck in some fresh night air to clear his head. His wrists are handcuffed to the water pipe. They're rubbed raw and blistering. His ankles are bound by ropes, and he's freezing because he is wearing only his army pants. They took his shoes and shirt right before the beating started.

His head flops back, resting on the cement wall. Savannah's sweet voice finds him, and he gets lost in his thoughts.

"Promise me you'll come back to me." Her dark eyes are flooded with tears. It's against all Army

and personal rules, but if this is what it takes to make the look go away, then he'll promise her the world.

"I promise, baby." He wraps his arms around her. "I want to hold you." She nods as he takes her hand, walking down the path.

"It's so pretty through here," she whispers, trying to break the sadness of the situation. "The forest just goes for miles and miles. It's an endless path to who knows where." She clears her throat. "So much freedom." He squeezes her hand. "Have you ever just wanted to follow the moonlight?"

He glances over to see the moon is casting a trail deep into the forest. "I have thought of that, many times, actually." They both walk, deep in thought.

Suddenly she stops dead in her tracks. "Run away with me."

His lips curl up as he brings their joined hands to his mouth and kisses her fingers. "I'd love nothing more than to run away with you, Savannah. But running won't make what I do for a living go away. It's a part of me." He wipes a stray tear off her trembling chin, soaking up this moment with her. "I'm nothing without you." He leans down, catching her lips and kissing her softly. "And you, baby, are the best part of me."

Drawing her lip in between her teeth, she nods. Letting out a long breath, she turns to gather herself.

"You want to head back?" She slowly shakes her head. "What do you want to do?"

She steps over to the edge of the cliff, looking down at the house. She spreads her arms out as wide as they can go.

"I want to fly," she whispers.

Cole pulls out his radio, watching her head tilt to look up at the sky. "Mark, you there?"

"Roger." Mark laughs over the radio.

"I need you to get Mike to bring me something."

Several minutes later Mike appears off to the side. "Have fun." He winks before he runs back down the path.

Cole grins as he walks over to Savannah, who is still lost in thought.

"Your wish is granted." Her eyes open then drop to what Cole is holding. "You said you wanted to fly."

The smile that runs across her lips is the sweetest thing. He takes a minute to let it etch into his memory.

He points the wooden toboggan down a clear path and tugs Savannah between his legs.

"You ready?"

She wraps his arms around her waist. "Ready."

He pushes off, and they start to move and pick up speed. Savannah's laugh echoes off the mountains, making him laugh. She jumps up and offers him a hand. He takes it, pulling her back down on his lap.

Something runs across her face and a tiny smile appears. "I didn't think it was possible."

"What?" he asks, confused.

"Possible to love you even more than I do right now."

"Move!" Someone shouts, making Cole jump. Savannah seems unfazed by the man yelling. Her lips are moving, but he can't hear her.

"Savannah?" he asks, nearly panicked. "What's going on?"

"Up!" the voice says again.

One minute he's with her, the next he's back in his room...

Men are shouting outside his door. He wipes the bead of sweat from his neck. A dream, a memory, a fantasy, whatever you want to call it, it's his and only his. They can't take that from him.

A voice makes his skin crawl as he turns and rests his back on the wall. Wincing from the cold, he slips back into another memory.

Everything changes once the video is made.

He is dragged into the room where a camera is pointing at a Mexican flag on the wall. He is positioned on his knees while the guy with the longhorn belt buckle, the one they call Raul, orders one of the men to leave. Moments later the man returns with a white guy in a Hawaiian print shirt and khakis. He drops him on the floor and nods at Raul. The guy looks either half dead or drugged.

Cole is trying to catch up when he sees Raul reaching for a machete. He can feel the blood drain from his face and swallows hard. A man comes over and inspects his neck, then does the same to the guy on the floor.

"Same," the man says to Raul.

"Good."

Than it hits Cole this is all being filmed, but why? He sees the red light go on, and they instruct Cole to stare into the camera. They turn on a bright light and aim it at him. He watches as Raul stands to his side and starts a speech. The camera travels down, and he sees the little red light go off. Someone grabs Cole and pulls him aside, shoving a pistol in his face. He watches in horror as they rip off the other man's shirt and hold him up.

"Not a word," the man warns, shaking the pistol at Cole.

The camera travels up Raul's waist then moves over to the man's neck, not showing any of his face. A moment later his throat is sliced open. Blood flies everywhere, including on Cole's arms and chest. The man turns and flops to the ground. The realization hits that this video is going to be seen by his family, but before he can even form another thought he's being dragged back into the closet and again handcuffed to the pipe.

He had heard The American come back, raging mad after hearing Raul made the video and sent it off without his knowledge. Clearly The American and Luka Donavan had nothing to do with the tape. In the days that followed, Cole had been driving himself crazy imagining all sorts of horrific scenarios of his family seeing what they thought was his beheading. He feels sick thinking of Savannah and her reaction to such a thing, let alone his parents.

Jerking awake after another terrible nightmare, Cole desperately runs his hands along the pipe to the ground and picks up the jug of water they threw at him the night before. He has been carefully sipping it, making sure he doesn't get sick by

Shattered

drinking it too fast. He winces as he moves, feeling the large open gash on his stomach. He knows it's probably getting infected in his filthy living conditions. Thankfully, they have been taking him outside to relieve himself. One time they didn't secure the blindfold properly, and Cole got a good look at his surroundings. He's been out enough times now to know what direction to head when he finally makes his move.

The door opens and The American steps inside the room, turning on the overhead light. He chucks a protein bar at Cole, and as he fumbles with numb fingers to pick it up, he sees it's one from the vest he was wearing the night they raided the house. Cole's stomach sinks as he realizes they went through his gear.

"So," The American says, smiling. "I'm gathering it just clicked for you that we found this," he holds up the picture, "tucked in the lining of your vest. Isn't there some rule that you're not supposed to carry anything that can lead us to your loved ones?" Cole jaw tightens as he glances at the picture of Savannah. "So Luka was right," he nods, "you're in love with the girl too." He smirks, glancing at the photo as his thumb brushes over her face. "What an interesting turn of events." He checks his watch then stands, studying Cole for a moment, then turns off the light and leaves.

Fuck me.

***

"Up!" a man yells at Cole, thinking he's asleep.

In fact, he was listening to the background sounds to see if other men are around. All is quiet.

Perfect.

The man kicks him in the leg. "I said up!" Cole's eyes slowly open.

The guy leans over and fumbles with the key to unlock the cuffs. His eyes are dilated and he looks strung out on something. Cole waits patiently while the man releases him. He needs to see if anyone is in the house. The man is so out of it he forgets to blindfold him, and Cole watches where he puts the cuff key after he links his other wrist. "Out." The man nudges him between his shoulder blades with his rifle.

He keeps his head down but notices two guys just as high nearly passed out on the couch, along with a tray lined with cocaine in front of them. One man looks over at them and grunts something about how it isn't the time to let the *gringo* out yet, but the man just urges Cole to keep moving. Cole peeks at the time on the wall and learns it's just past midnight. Lots of darkness left to use to his advantage.

"Tree." The guy points to the nearest tree. "Hurry."

Cole nods then glances over the man's shoulder like he sees something. The guard turns quickly, and Cole wraps his arms around the man's neck and holds on tightly. Cole hooks his leg around the man's; holding him closer to his body he flexes with all his might finally feeling the pop he is waiting for. The guard goes limp and falls to the ground, slipping from his grasp. Cole quickly plucks the key from the guard's pocket, frees himself from the cuffs and tosses them into the shadows. He snags the gun and rolls the man into the brush, all the while watching the door for the two other men. They don't show. Just as he pushes off the man's body, he feels something square in his pocket. He pulls out a phone.

Perfect.

With the gun flung over his shoulder and the phone secure in his pocket, Cole runs into the thin wooded area and heads north toward the mountain where he can find high ground and good cover. He runs and runs and runs, letting the stars guide him. Breathing is everything; you need to control your breathing to keep your heart rate steady so you can run longer. Luckily for Cole, he has long legs which allow him to sprint through the brush. After about forty minutes of flat-out running, he slows, feeling pain deep inside his gut. He stops and holds onto a tree. His hands reach down and feel blood soaking the top of his pants. *Mind over matter.* What he needs is some clean water and a piece of clothing to wrap his midsection.

Something catches his attention off to his left, and he drops to the ground, swinging his gun in front of him and scanning the tree trunks. It's dark, and the woods are thick in some areas, but Cole can spot a panther stalking its prey before it can spot him.

A familiar whistle breaks through the silent night. It takes Cole a few moments to recognize the tone. He squints when he hears it again.

"Raven One," a male voice calls out in perfect

English, "I'm a scout for Eagle Eye One."

Holy shit, he's a fucking scout for Frank!

"Name?" Cole calls out, still keeping his gun raised.

"Staff Sergeant Mills, Colonel."

"Show yourself." There's a rustling sound, then a man dressed in dark clothes appears, holding his hands up. Cole grips the gun tightly but lowers it as soon as he sees the man lift his shirt, showing a U.S. Army tattoo confirming which unit he's in. He's definitely part of Frank's team. "You alone, Mills?" Cole asks, allowing himself to sag against the tree.

"No, sir. Sergeant Hahn is on high ground while I came down here to find you."

"You were watching the house?"

"Yes, sir." Mills nods and comes closer as he checks the time.

"You expecting someone?"

"Yes, sir. Blackstone is on their way."

"Wait," Cole says, shifting his weight. "Blackstone is on their way here?" Mills nods. "When?"

"Should be arriving in twenty."

Well, fuck me sideways.

"Let me see your radio, Mills." Mills hands it to him, saying they're on channel six. Cole holds it to his mouth and clicks the button. "Blackstone One to Blackstone Two; do you copy?" Seven long seconds go by before he hears him.

"Blackstone Two to Blackstone One; your voice never sounded so sweet, brother." Cole grins at Mark's comment. "Meet at Eagle Eye Three's lookout point."

Shattered

"Copy that, Blackstone Two, meeting at Eagle Eye Three's lookout point." He hands his radio to Mills and nods toward the trees. "Lead the way."

"Yes, sir." Mills hesitates then reaches into his pants pocket, handing Cole a small pill in a plastic wrap. Cole shakes his head, not needing anything to cloud his judgment until he's back on U.S. soil. They head toward the mountains until halfway up Cole pulls Mills to the ground. A spotlight swipes the edge of the mountain; Cole spots it coming from a Land Rover about two miles from them. He signals for Mills to hand him his radio and clicks the button several times until he hears clicking back. He slips the radio in his pocket and cautions Mills to stay low but keep moving. They reach the top just as he hears the chopper blades off in the distance and his radio clicking Morse code at him. It's Mark wondering if they still have company. He clicks back confirming they're several hundred yards behind them and to be prepared.

Mills slides between two rocks and into a small hole which offers a panoramic view of where Cole had been held captive. He removes a small box of rations, water, a blanket, and his duffel bag.

Eying up Mill's duffel, Cole looks at him. "How long have you been here, Mills?"

"A week, sir. We got word someone was being held down there, so Frank had us watching the house. Hahn and I thought it was you, but given the video, we figured it must be someone else. We didn't say anything. We had to be sure it was you before we could report to Eagle Eye One." Mills cocks his machine gun, getting ready to fire. "The day they took you outside without your shirt, we were able to confirm it was you." Mills nods to Cole's tattoo. "Your ink was a dead giveaway." He hands Cole another gun, then motions to head back out into the open.

The chopper is just landing as they come to the clearing. Mills moves over the edge and signals the Cartels are close. Cole nods to the chopper when Mills is suddenly flung backward from the force of two bullets to the side of his torso. Cole leaps forward, grabbing Mills by his arms and pulling him back toward the chopper as it lands. Mark suddenly appears at his side.

"We have to go!" Mark shouts, clutching Mill's other arm and helping Cole pull him inside the chopper.

"We need to pick up the other scout!" Cole yells as they signal the chopper to leave.

"It's too risky!"

"The other scout!" Cole commands, catching a glimpse of his father. They exchange a look.

"The other scout," Daniel calls out to the pilot. He gives Cole a tight smile, then drops his gaze to Cole's bloody midsection. "You all right, son?"

"Yeah." Cole reaches out and grabs his father's shoulder, giving it a light squeeze. The pilot radios to Frank and gets Hahn's coordinates. In minutes they are landing to pick up Hahn. He hops in and immediately leans over Mills, who is holding his hand over one of the wounds. He looks at Keith and gives him a slight nod, thanking him for looking after his partner till he got there.

"Hit it!" Cole's voice rings through the chopper

and makes everyone jump to positions. Immediately three small bombs hit the house where Cole had been held.

Cole leans back into the seat, finally letting the pain sink in. Mark crawls over and has a look at Cole's cut.

"This is a bad one, Cole." He sees Mark glance at his father. He nods, knowing he'll need staples and some seriously strong antibiotics. His eyelids feel heavy and he slowly drifts off.

Cole barely remembers being lifted out of the chopper. He has only a vague recall of the doctor telling him what needed to be done and of getting the staples across his torso. He was told he had a cracked skull and therefore a concussion. He welcomed sleep when it came, bringing with it dreams of holding Savannah.

I kept my promise, baby.

Chapter Two

Cole swings his feet so they dangle over the edge of the bed and attempts to get up. He's been in this private hospital room in North Dakota for two days, and it's been long enough. His torso still burns like hell and his head feels like someone is in there enjoying themselves by smashing his skull relentlessly with a sledgehammer, but he knows he needs to get up and get moving.

"Whoa...!" The spunky little redheaded nurse holds up her hands, coming into the room. "Where do you think you're going, big boy?" He's known Molly for a few years now; this is where the guys come if they need medical attention when they're injured. They have to get clearance to go back to the house. She may be a sweet woman, but she has a will of iron, so he knows he has to tread lightly.

"I need to go, Molly. I've been here long enough and I feel a lot better." He reaches for his shirt, slipping it over his head with a grunt.

Her hands go to her hips. "I haven't cleared you yet."

"So clear me."

"Cole, you know I can't do that. We're still worried about your head."

"Head's fine."

"Cole," she scolds him.

Frustrated, Cole argues. "Molly, you can either clear me or make my day shitty by having me fill out more paperwork than I already have, but either way I'm leaving."

She sighs and studies him then smiles tightly. "Give me ten minutes."

The door swings open and Cole's father walks in holding two coffees.

"Maybe you can convince him to stay," Molly grumbles as she leaves the room.

Cole shakes his head. "Don't even start, Dad. I need to get home."

Daniel hands Cole his coffee and sits in a chair watching him struggle to pull on his pants. "I agree we should get you home."

Something in his voice causes Cole to stop his attempt to button his fly, and he looks at his father. "What happened? Is Savannah all right? Is she hurt?"

Daniel takes a deep breath and runs his finger along the rim of his cup before turning back with a tired look. "We thought she was asleep in her room, but she came down when we were looking at the tape."

"Fuck." Cole rubs his aching head as he slowly sits down, letting that piece of knowledge sink in along with the memory of the poor guy who was unlucky enough to be his double in the video.

"Yeah, it was, ahhhh…" Daniel clears his throat. "A lot has happened since you've been gone. If you're feeling well enough, I think we should get you back. Damage control is going to take some time. She has been through a terrible shock."

Cole sighs then winces from the pain. "Does she know I'm all right?"

"We thought it was best not to say anything until we physically got you home. We didn't want to add any more ups and downs to the emotional rollercoaster she's already on."

"I feel like you're not telling me everything, Dad. You've never lied to me before, so please don't start now."

Daniel leans forward and rests his elbows on his knees. "No, son, I'm not lying. There are just some things that aren't my place to discuss with you."

Cole watches his father for a moment, seeing something like pain flash over his face. It doesn't take much to figure out that something is up, and it isn't good. It has his stomach in a knot. "Just tell me, is she all right?"

"Yes, she's all right," his father says, standing up, "but there are so many questions that need answers, Cole. First we need to get you out of here. While we're waiting for Molly to get your clearance, you need to call your mother." He hands a cell phone to Cole.

"Yeah," Cole takes the phone, "of course."

"I'll be right outside."

Cole dials and tries to think about what to say.

"Daniel?" His mother's worried voice rings through the phone.

Shattered

Tears threaten Cole's eyes as he takes in a deep breath and speaks. "Mom?" There is the longest pause, then a quiet sob on the other end.

"Oh, honey," she manages to get out.

"I'm okay, Mom, truly. A few bangs and scrapes, but all things considered, I'm fine. Dad is here with me and we're heading out shortly. We should be home by late tonight."

"All right, son, I…" Her voice shakes.

"Mom, please don't tell Savi that I'm coming. Dad's right to keep it quiet…just until I make it back. Some things happened while I was gone and—"

"Of course, honey, I agree. She has been through so much…" She starts crying again. "Get Dad to call me later to give me a better idea of your arrival time. I love you, Cole, so very much."

"I love you too, Mom. I'll see you soon." He wants to talk to Savannah, to tell her he's alive and okay, but something tells him that he should have her in his arms first, just in case. He feels torn, but with the way his parents are acting, he knows things aren't right.

"Well, you look like shit." Mark grins, bursting into the room in typical Mark style. *God, he missed him.* "You ready to go, or are you going to fake your injury some more? Molly's a hot little number, hey?"

"Really?" Cole rolls his eyes while Mark tosses him a piece of gum. He doesn't think before popping it in his mouth until his tongue is invaded with a nasty taste. "Oh shit!"

"What?" Mark shrugs, looking positively

delighted that he got Cole to eat it. "It's called Cool Cola." Cole makes a face and spits it into the trash. "You now owe me two pieces of Hubba Bubba, dude."

"Yech." He reaches for his water, swirling it around his mouth trying to relieve his taste buds.

Mark laughs. "Come on, the chopper is waiting. It will take us to the mountains, then we'll drive the rest of the way. Changing it up, just in case."

"Good plan."

***

Savannah

I notice Sue's mood has changed from this morning. She has actually eaten a whole meal, seems to be interacting with people, and her usual demeanor of looking like she's off in space is replaced by someone more like she used to be. *Lucky her.* I, on the other hand, feel like an empty shell. I try hard to act somewhat normal just so people will stop hovering over me. I feel like I did when I first arrived at the house—completely out of place, full of pain and not sure where I belong. I pick up my untouched plate and place it on the counter. I can feel Abigail and June watching me. I turn toward the hallway and make my way to the front door, shrugging into my coat and boots and heading outside.

It's lightly snowing and everything is silent. As expected, the front door opens and closes and I hear footsteps behind me.

Please, go away.

"I just need a minute, Derek,"

I'm so tired.

"First, don't ever refer to me as *that* selfish ass," Mike says, approaching me. "And second, I just wanted to go for some fresh air too." I roll my eyes, but I find his company welcome. Mike has been busy the last two days hiding away in Cole's—his office. Oh god, even thinking his name makes me shake and want to curse at the sky. I really am losing it.

"He's not that bad, you know," I whisper as we make our way through the fluffy snow.

"Who, Derek?"

"Yes." I nod. "Derek has been friendly and respectful."

"Well, that's good," Mike says with mild sarcasm. I let it go, too tired to take it on.

"Let's go this way." He points toward my favorite spot up in the mountains.

"Sure." I follow mindlessly, my boots crunching in the snow. It used to be one of my favorite sounds, but now, not so much.

"I know it's late, and it's the last thing you ever want to talk about, but I'm sorry about your baby, Savi."

I feel like I've just taken a punch to my stomach, but I manage to hold it together. "Thanks, Mike," I whisper, truly knowing he's a good friend. I let my mind wander as we reach the top and look over the beautiful landscape. I let out a long, shaky breath. "Our baby was the only little bit I had left of Cole." I swallow around the lump in my throat. "It's all my fault it didn't live." Mike's arm wraps around my shoulder. "It was the only thing I had left, Mike." I start to cry quietly as he holds me. He removes his arm, checking the time on his watch.

"No, it's not," he whispers.

I wiggle his arm off me. "I don't want to hear about having faith and God does things for a reason. God does mean, cruel things sometimes—" I feel my anger rise and am about to take my hurt out on my friend when I hear an engine and see a pair of headlights coming our way. The guys must be back from their latest mission.

"Sorry, Savannah, you won't get a speech from me. I don't believe in God." Mike smiles. "I believe in karma and the big bang."

"Good," I respond, but his growing grin is making me uneasy. The SUV pulls up and Mike starts walking toward it.

"Come on, Savi, let's greet the guys. I'm sure they've had a tough trip."

"Yeah, just give me a minute." I wipe my cold face free of tears. God, I am sick of crying! I stick my icy hands in my jacket pockets and try to get my head clear. The last thing the guys need to see is 'fragile Savannah' right now. I turn on my heel take a step forward and stop dead in my tracks.

What?

Cole is standing a few feet from me wearing a black jacket, a hat, and army pants. I shake my head in disbelief, reminding myself to breathe. It can't be...

"Savannah," he whispers, giving me a half smile. I look over at the guys, who are all grinning like

Shattered

fools. Cole starts toward me. I notice he has a small limp, I see his face, his unsure smile—it feels surreal. I can't move.

"But I watched you die," I whisper as he reaches out and cups my face. His hands feel so warm. "I'm dreaming." I start to sob. "This is a fucking dream, this is cruel." I start to panic, as I've experienced moments over the last few days where I could almost believe none of it had happened, only to realize with dread that it had.

"No, baby," he leans in, "this is fucking real." He smashes his lips to mine, making me feel him. I reach around his neck and deepen the kiss, just wanting to feel something, even if only for a moment. His thumb brushes away my tears as he slowly pulls back, and I see tears in his eyes as well. "Hi, baby." My hands move through his hair, over his face, down to his shoulders. I let out a giddy laugh, but it gets caught in my throat. I shake my head, not sure what to say as the shock begins taper slightly, so I go with the obvious.

"Hi," I say back. "How?"

He shakes his head, staring deep into my eyes as if *I'm* not real.

"Let's get inside and I'll tell you everything, okay?" He winces when he lowers his arms.

"Are you all right?" I step back, inspecting him. He is obviously in pain, but he looks intact.

"I am now." He takes my hand, threading his fingers through mine. He raises them to his mouth, kissing our joined hands. Tears stream down my face as I take in that he's actually standing right here in front of me. My Cole, my love, my reason for living is back.

We walk in silence, and the guys follow behind us. His hand continues to squeeze mine. I have no idea what to say or what to think, but I can feel my heart thawing just a little.

Sue flies out the door. I let go of his hand as she wraps her arms around her son. She is crying happy tears. Abigail and June do the same, all taking their turn to ensure he's alive and well. I step back a few steps, feeling so confused. I bump into Daniel, who smiles down at me as he gives me a side hug.

"It's just shock, honey. You'll come around soon. Give yourself a moment to let it sink in."

I turn away from everyone as I gather myself for like the eighth time today. Lord, what I wouldn't do to have a handle on my emotions. I feel his hand find mine again, and I turn and see him looking down at me with a questioning expression.

"Don't let go again, okay?" He gives me a tug toward him, kissing my forehead as he leads me into the house.

We all gather together in the living room to celebrate his return, everyone laughing and talking. I can't seem to pull myself out of the shock and sadness that still has a firm hold on me. What's wrong with me? I should be ecstatic, but instead I'm swimming with a hundred different emotions. I try to interact with everyone. Mark hands me his special Marcus Martini. I take it and thank him, but I just stare at it.

"Okay, honey, let's hear the story," Sue says after everyone has quieted down. "I need to know, as I'm sure everyone else does."

Cole nods then takes a long sip of his beloved brandy and squeezes my hand. "Let's see, the last thing I can remember is keeping watch as the guys left the house. We needed to get out of there. Mark and Paul needed a medic. I must have been hit on the back of the head. I woke to someone taking an electric—" He stops himself and looks at me. "They roughed me up a bit, wanting to get the location of the house. They kept me handcuffed to a pipe in a small room, fed me just enough to hold on. This went on for a while until The American showed up. We had some words, and finally he got tired of me not answering his questions. The days kind of mesh together, but mostly they just pumped me for information. One night The American left the house, and that's when the video was made by a man named Raul."

I start to shake. I feel it start in my legs then travel up my spine through my arms and hands, and my teeth start to chatter. I sit my untouched drink down since it's spilling over my hand. Keith catches my eye, but I pretend not to notice.

"So if that wasn't you on the tape," Paul says, squinting like he's not really sure he wants to know, "who was it?"

I feel Cole's grip tighten. "They had a guy already drugged. His build was similar to mine. I don't know who the poor bastard was, but we need to find out to let his family know. They obviously didn't plan it well, as they didn't catch my tattoo." Cole bends his head down, breathing deeply. "It's an understatement to say that was a pretty bad day."

"Yeah, it was." Mark looks over at me. I quickly

wipe a tear away, shaking my head at him.

Cole looks down at me, then at everyone in the room. "Look, everyone, thanks. I'll fill you in more tomorrow, but right now I need some time with Savannah, and we all need sleep." He stands and pulls me up with him.

When we reach the bedroom, he takes in the couch that's made up like a bed against the wall and looks at me.

"Keith," I whisper, moving to the bathroom and attempting to tuck my feelings away. Once I'm washed and ready for bed, I head back out and see Cole sitting on the edge of the bed, staring at me. He holds out his hand, reaching for mine. He pulls me between his legs and looks up into my eyes. My heart squeezes when I think about how I almost ended my life, thinking he was gone forever.

"I know this is really confusing, and it kills me to realize you saw that tape, but I'm here, and I'm fine." I swallow hard, needing to be strong. I run my hands through his hair.

"You kept your promise," I say through a tight throat.

His mouth curls up and his eyes crinkle. "A promise is a promise." He frowns when he studies my face. "What happened while I was gone?" I try, I really do, to get the words off my tongue, but I stay silent. Instead I reach for the hem of his shirt until his hands stop mine. "Savannah, please." I shake my head no, and he doesn't push…yet.

I hear him flinch as he raises his arms over his head, and a moment later I see why. My hands fly over my mouth as I gasp. A huge bandage is

Shattered

wrapped around his mid-section.

"You're hurt!"

"I'm all right," he hisses. "I'm just exhausted."

"No, you're not all right." I carefully stand him up. Undoing his pants, I help him lie back on the bed and crawl up by his head. I lean against the massive headboard as he shifts to rest his head on my legs.

"What was it like?" I ask, wanting to compare what he went through with what I had.

He sighs and closes his eyes. "Frustrating not being able to defend myself physically. It was all mental, but thankfully I had something to focus on." His hand slides over my thigh. "I think the hardest part was knowing I was alive but you all didn't."

"Yeah," is all I can say. The lump in my throat has returned.

I run my fingers through his silky hair methodically until I hear his breathing become even. My mind is running a marathon, but I cannot make sense of any of it yet. I'm still off on the sidelines of it all, too exhausted to even try. I glance at the clock and see it's two in the morning. Unable to settle yet, I slip Cole gently off my lap, slide off the bed, and head downstairs.

I lean back on the cool bricks after lighting the fireplace in the living room, set a large glass of brandy in front of me and try to take a sip, but my stomach rejects the liquor. Everything becomes a blur as my eyes fill and tears spill over my cheeks. I rest the tiny teddy on my lap like one would do with a child and cling to the little silver frame wishing with all my heart I had listened when people told me to calm down. How could I be so blind? So selfish? I killed our baby.

"It's not your fault."

My head snaps up, and I find Keith watching me from the kitchen. He comes over and takes a seat next to me. I shift so he has some room.

"Yes, it is." I sniff, swimming in a sea of emotions. "All of this is my fault, but the fact that I lost—" I shake my head and try to clear the terrible images flickering in front of me. "To top it off, I had a—" I can't say the word so I skip over it, "to my head and almost—"

"You had what to your head?" Both Keith and I jump at the sound of Cole's husky voice. I slowly look over, seeing him standing there in his sweat pants, bare feet, and nothing else. His face looks angry and confused as he takes a few steps toward us. "Someone better tell me what the hell happened while I was gone."

Keith reaches over and squeezes my shoulder as he stands up, nodding at Cole. Cole takes his seat and watches me closely. I take a deep breath through my nose, knowing this is the moment when I have to break his heart, as mine is broken, to tell him what we had and then lost—our child.

"What's that?" He points at the teddy his father gave me. I hand it to him and watch his eyes roll over the little name stitched into its army jacket. His gaze flicks up to me, making my lip tremble. I slowly turn the small frame around and show him the ultrasound picture. "Are you...?" He looks at my stomach.

"Was," I correct him through streaming hot tears.

"I was five weeks till the day the video arrived." His eyes widen then drop slowly and he shakes his head. He then covers his mouth with one hand.

I want to scream, sob, and run away from all of this pain. I can see I'm about to break him, by chipping away a piece of an already battered soul. It's just not right. *So much of me is shattered.*

"I'm so sorry, Cole."

His red glossy eyes shoot up to mine. "No, no." He kneels down in front of me, holding my hands. "No, baby, *I'm* so sorry you went through all of this without me. I-I..." His voice catches. "I can't believe you were pregnant with our baby."

Here it goes.

I pull back to look at him. "I don't know how you feel about this, but I was going to keep it."

"No," he wipes my cheeks dry and moves to sit next to me, "*we* were going to keep it." My heart swells as I fill him in on all the details, like how Sue and Daniel were the only ones to know, then Keith because I wanted him to keep my secret until he returned safely. I take him through the moments when I miscarried, sobbing quietly as I share the details with him. The whole time he holds me tightly, giving my head light kisses. Then we sit in silence for a while, grieving together. His sobs are hard to hear, but he needs to let it out. It's hard seeing someone who is normally so strong crumble in front of you.

Suddenly he stops moving. "What did you have held to your head?" I try to move, but his grip won't let me.

"I—I found your gun behind your night table."

His entire body starts to vibrate, and I spit out the words in fear I won't be able to finish. "I lost you, I lost our baby, and I still don't know who's behind my kidnapping. I had no reason to live. I just wanted to be with my family." The words are falling out of my mouth with no filter. "Then Keith's cell phone rang, and I hesitated, and he saw me. He...he talked to me, helped me off the ledge." I just keep talking as Cole's eyes bore into me. "It was a pretty dark time, Cole, the darkest I've ever been." I shift to look up at him. His eyes are squeezed shut now, and I move to kiss his jaw. "I won't say I'm sorry about it, Cole, because I didn't know you were alive, and if I am to be honest with myself, I think I would have tried again. But now you're here, but the baby isn't, and I'm trying to tell myself it wasn't meant to be, but it still hurts." The painful lump grows larger. "It hurts so damn bad, but having you back makes me see we can get through this if we—"

He suddenly leans forward, capturing my mouth with his. I know the drive behind the kiss is fear, so I follow, letting him take the lead. He needs to feel in control, and I'm willing to hand over the reins. I am too emotionally exhausted to be strong right now.

"Come back to bed," he whispers. "I need to hold you."

He leads us upstairs and we climb into bed. I shift carefully so as not to hurt his staples, and wrap my arm over his chest and my leg over his waist. I burrow my face in his neck, and it starts to sink in that he is really back. I feel his chest rise and fall, and with a deep sigh his fingers find mine, entwining them.

"Do you hurt?" he asks in a tight voice.

"Not in the way you're thinking."

Just my heart.

I hear him swallow loudly and clear his throat. I know it is all hitting him now. We lie tangled, letting each be strong for the other while we take turns to grieve.

"I love you, Savannah," he whispers.

"I love you too, Cole."

Chapter Three

Cole

Cole wakes to an empty bed, noticing Savannah laid out his painkillers and a bottle of water for him. He downs the two pills and heads for a much-needed shower. It takes him longer than normal to get dressed, which is annoying as he also has to change the dressing on his staples. The cut is healing well and the infection is gone; he just has to wait a week before he can get the staples pulled. He makes his way downstairs and into the kitchen where Abigail is baking something and talking quietly to his mother.

"How'd you sleep, dear?" his mother asks him, giving him a kiss on the cheek. She looks him over silently, probably to satisfy herself that he is really here and in one piece.

"Fine." He yawns and reaches for the coffee.

Keith enters the kitchen and comes up next to Cole, looking out the window.

"Thanks, Keith," Cole says quietly, "for taking

care of her when I couldn't and for stopping her—"

"Don't thank me. Savi is like a sister. I'm just glad you're back."

Speaking of her... "Do you know where she is?"

"Dr. Roberts."

"Really?" Abigail and Sue both say at the same time.

"Yeah, I know." Keith turns to them.

Cole looks around the room, seeing their faces. "Why are we surprised?"

Sue shakes her head. "She stopped the sessions after we found out you were…gone. I guess she just needed some time to sort things out on her own."

Cole leans back against the island, feeling beat even though he just got up. He checks the time, as he has a meeting with the guys in his office in fifteen. His stomach flutters when he hears her voice down the hallway.

"It's therapeutic, Savannah," he hears Dr. Roberts say. "Sometimes things that used to bring you comfort can still help you heal new wounds and old wounds too."

"Maybe," she sniffs. "It's just it makes me think of him, and it's hard to know where to place those feelings right now."

"I understand and that makes perfect sense. Try to pull from the old happy memories. You need to find a release, and this sounds like a perfect way to do it."

"I prefer Mark's way better," she huffs, rounding the corner.

"You'll get the poor guy fired, if Logan finds out." Dr. Roberts smiles when he sees everyone staring at them as they enter the kitchen. "Hi, Cole, it's great to see you looking well." He extends his hand for a shake. Before Cole leans back, he reaches for Savannah and guides her to his side, needing her to ground him. She nuzzles and molds herself to him.

"How was the session?" Cole asks.

"Good." Dr. Roberts smiles at Savannah. "But I'm sorry, I must get going."

"I'll walk you out." Abigail jumps to her feet.

Cole leans down and kisses Savannah on her head. "I have a video conference, but will you come see me afterward?"

"Sure." She gives him a smile, but he can see she is raw from her session. She leans up and gives him a kiss.

"Oh, Savannah," Abigail holds up a spoon full of cookie dough, "can you taste this? Something's missing."

Savannah's face goes funny as she moves to Abigail's side. She runs her fingers delicately over the top of the red Mixmaster.

"Something wrong, dear?"

"My mother," she whispers through a tiny smile, "she used to have one just like this. Cherry red." Her eyes light up. "I haven't seen one in years."

Abigail kisses her cheek, making Savannah notice everyone is staring at her. She takes the spoon and tastes the dough. "A pinch of cocoa powder."

"That's it!" Abigail shouts, giving her a hug. "Maybe I should leave the baking to you."

Cole smiles at the interaction between Savannah

Shattered

and Abigail, and leaves the kitchen to head to the conference room.

"How's the...?" Mark points to his side as he takes a seat at a large table in a conference room downstairs.

"Annoying," Cole grunts out, feeling the burn from within his deep cut.

"I bet it is." He winks. Classic Mark, he's always thinking about food or getting laid.

Guess that's not such a bad obsession.

Daniel, Keith, Paul, and John take their seats around the table while Cole fires up his laptop and gets Frank on the conference call. His face flashes on the large screen on the wall, and Cole centers the microphone between them.

"Logan, good to have you back." Frank nods as he rustles some papers on his desk.

"Good to be back. How is Mills doing?"

"All things considered, he'll be just fine. Has a long road to recovery, though."

Cole spends the next hour going over every detail of what happened. Meanwhile, Frank is emailing his snapshots of the two main men were who were helping The American, and one recent one of Luka Donavan, still in Mexico.

"Strange that he's still there," Cole says, leaning back in his seat. "I would have thought he'd be hightailing it back to New York to warn the mayor I'm gone. They know they screwed up by telling their dirty little secret." All the men look at Cole, clearly wondering what he's referring to. "Luka and Lynn," he explains, "her best friend and family friend, are the two who are behind this whole shit storm."

"What?" Mark nearly chokes on his coffee. "You mean to tell me that Savannah's only real family, the woman she talks about all the time, is behind her kidnapping?"

"Yes." Cole nods. "Not only was she behind it, but she hired a guy to pose as a potential client for the company to take Savannah out and to get her home at the right time for those savages to take her."

"What about her father?" Frank asks, fishing for a lead. "Anything there?"

"According to Donavan, when her father got word she had been kidnapped and Luka was behind it, he decided his little pistol was better off staying with *Los Sirvientes Del Diablo* than to be there with him getting in his way." Cole makes a face. "He is up for reelection, and with his daughter being kidnapped his votes skyrocketed. He knew she was eventually going to be killed, and dear old Dad did nothing about it. He completely wrote her off."

"This is insane," Keith mutters, getting up from his chair. "How do you tell her something like this?"

"You don't," Frank says, moving toward the camera. "Until we have proof of this, Savannah is not going to hear about it. She's been through enough already."

Cole glances at his father, who is watching him. His father shakes his head, agreeing with Frank's decision.

Shit.

Cole drops his gaze, knowing it's best right now

to keep quiet. She's been through too much.

Mark turns to Frank. "Okay, so what now?"

"Now, we start to dig."

***

Savannah

I lie down on the floor and shimmy myself under the branches of the Christmas tree. It was something I always did as a child, looking up at the lights and enjoying how they lit up the needles and made it look so pretty. It is a peaceful thing I haven't done in a long time.

Scoot finds me in a matter of seconds and jams up next to my side, purring for affection. His big brown eyes close as I rub his belly.

I take a deep breath through my nose and let the smell take me away to a childhood memory where my mother and I chopped off a few branches to make a door to the snow fort we had worked on all afternoon. Dad came out with a tray of hot chocolates with marshmallows, and we all crammed into the fort and enjoyed our snack.

I hear a click and bend my head to see who it is. I find Keith holding a camera and grinning at me. He kneels down and turns the camera around so I can see the picture. I laugh when I see Scoot's and my legs sticking out from the bottom of the tree.

"Now that's funny." He offers me a hand to stand. "Cole asked if I could find you to see if you'd join him for lunch. He's just finishing up some paperwork in his office."

"The man never stops, does he?"

"Nope."

Hearing my heels click on the wooden floor makes me shake my head. I didn't think I would be happy walking back to his office again. The door is already open, so I poke my head around and see him, arms crossed, standing in front of his huge floor to ceiling window. He looks powerful and strong, making me grin as I step further into the room. He's still here with me.

He must have heard me because he slowly turns and graces me with a smile that hits me right in the center of my heart. "I was beginning to think you stood me up," he teases.

"I was just admiring the view." I make my way over to him and tuck myself into his side. "What were you just thinking about?"

His grip tightens on my hip but he doesn't say anything for a moment then kisses my head and asks if I am hungry.

"I am." I give him a wink.

"First…" He laughs, heading over to his desk and pulling out a square, flat box. He comes back and hands it to me. "Merry Christmas."

I slide it out of his hands and pull at the bow. I peel back the top and my breathing nearly stops. "How did you get this?"

"I have my ways." He leans in and grants me a soft kiss on the cheek. I swallow hard as my fingers stroke the record signed by Flat Street Tony. The very record that used to hang on my living room wall. But even more surprising is what is under it. My chin begins quiver.

"Oh," I whisper.

"I hope it's okay that I—"

"*Yes*," I laugh through a sob, "this one was my favorites of us." My heart lodges in my throat as I hold the 8x10 photograph of my mother and me, when I was ten, at a carnival. "Thank you Cole, truly it means the world to me." I smile up at him, feeling my love for this man growing more and more. "I can't believe you were able to get these for me!"

"I'll do anything to put that smile on your face, baby."

"That I don't doubt."

We settle in on the couch and eat our lunch and make small talk, but I can sense he has something to tell me.

"I have to leave in three days," he finally blurts out.

My heart jumps out of my chest. I know it would run right out the door if it could, just to avoid any more pain. He must sense this, because his hands grab mine quickly.

"It's not what you think. Team Blackstone is going to help with a special training exercise for the Green Berets." I feel my body go slack, allowing my heart to slowly recover. "Normally we'd be heading to North Carolina to Camp Mackall, but due to the sheer volume of candidates this year, we're doing the training at Camp Green Water here in Montana."

"I didn't know you guys helped out with the training."

"We don't have to, but we volunteer our time.

Plus I'm looking for a new recruit. Derek won't be staying on for much longer, and nothing is better than a fresh soldier I can mold."

"Derek is leaving?" I feel kind of sad. We have become friends over these last few weeks.

"No, not really." His eyes darken. "Frank has another position for him. He's a good solider, but he doesn't fit if he isn't trusted."

I want to argue but I decide against it. Cole makes logical decisions, so if Derek is to leave, it's for a good reason. "How long will you be gone?"

"Two weeks."

"Oh." My stomach twists.

He squeezes my hand. "I'm only going to be thirty minutes from here."

My eyebrows shoot up. "Really?"

"Yes, will you come visit me?"

"Can I?"

"Yes." He grins. "I don't want to go very long without seeing you, Savi."

I swallow hard, trying to sort out my nerves. "Me either."

***

"Six! Five! Four! Three! Two! One! *Happy New Year!*" everyone shouts, raising champagne flutes in the air.

I glance over and see Dr. Roberts sneak a quick kiss from Abigail. Mark sees it too. He rolls his eyes and looks away, muttering something about "that better be all he's expecting tonight."

I turn my attention to Cole, who has a wicked

Shattered

grin on his face. "Psssst," I whisper as I sit my glass down on the mantel and flick my finger in his direction. "This is the part where you kiss me."

He steps closer. "Then a kiss, Ms. Miller, you shall receive." He quickly grabs my head with one hand and the other runs up the length of my spine. With one fluid motion he dips and kisses me until I am breathless. My world tilts as his lips work magic, waking up every single nerve in my body. When he pulls away I realize everyone is clapping for us. I am thankful it is dark, because I feel my face turns at least three shades of red at that moment.

Cole chuckles as he pulls me to my feet.

"I didn't realize you were such a romantic, Colonel." That is a lie, but I can't think of anything else to say. I run my hand through my hair, taking a moment to calm myself. I pick up my glass and peer down into the empty flute. "Cole?"

"Yes?"

"Do you think you could help me with something?"

"Of course, what's up?"

"Can we speak in your office?" I start to walk.

He reaches for my hand and we head for his office. He punches in the code and lets me enter first.

"You want something from the bar?" he asks, walking over to pour himself a brandy.

"No." I pause by his desk and slip my dress off my shoulders, letting it fall to the floor. I step out and hop onto his desk, wearing a black and red lace bra, matching cheeky panties, and my black heels.

"I had something else in mind."

"Oh, yeah, what's that?" he asks as he turns to look at me. His jaw drops as his eyes rake down me and a shameless grin spreads across his lips.

"You on top of me on your desk." I pat the surface then lean back and rest on my arms. "Come bang in the New Year, baby." I grin, feeling oddly bold, but that's what Cole does to me, and I love it.

In three strides he's in front of me with his shirt off, both hands on my knees, gazing down at me.

"How did I ever get so lucky?" he whispers. "Will I hurt you?"

I reach for his hand and pull him down so he is close to me. "Cole, I'm fine. You won't hurt me. Nothing was damaged there." I arch my breasts into his chest, reach for his belt buckle, and yank it open. "I need to feel you."

Cole stands up, pulling his pants down and kicking them out of the way. He reaches under my knees and pulls my butt to the end of the desk. He leans down and kisses my stomach up to my bra and stops at my neck.

"I will never tire of feeling your silky skin," he says between kisses. "I love the way you smell."

"Cole," I whisper as I run my hands across his strong back. My heartbeat is a hammer in my chest.

"The way you say my name is like it is made solely for your sweet lips."

I hear a ripping sound, and my panties sail over my head. I can feel him resting outside my opening; it is a maddening feeling.

"Co—"

He pushes gently into me, and the slow friction

makes my head flop back and my back arch high.

"My sweet Savannah," his husky voice flows out across my chest, "you're like a dream I never want to wake up from."

He shifts so he is in deep, staring down at me. His eyes are incredibly dark and possessive. His lips brush over mine, muttering something I can't make out.

He leans back to stand, gripping my hips, and makes slow and sweet love to me, and the entire time his eyes stay locked with mine.

Chapter Four

Cole

Cole stands fully dressed in his gear, watching over sixty-three men low crawl through a sea of mud. It's cold inside the warehouse, but it doesn't matter. These men need to be able to handle anything thrown at them.

"There's been talk you're looking for a recruit."

"Major Anderson," Cole nods, "nice to see you again."

"You too, Colonel." He crosses his arms as he stands next to Cole. "Any men caught your attention?"

Cole smirks, not wanting it to be known that he is indeed looking. It's been five days of hell for these men. They've gotten maybe twenty-eight hours of sleep total.

"I have three if you're interested," Anderson says quietly. Cole doesn't bite; he continues to watch his own prospect. "Forty-three, eleven, and fifty-nine."

Shattered

Cole scans the men's arms and finds the three Anderson pointed out. Fifty-nine is already on his radar. His name is Captain Terrance Roth, from Texas. He's thirty and one tough son of a bitch. He'd be perfect to work under Mike, since Cole wants Keith to join Blackstone. Keith has proven time and time again that he should be on Cole's team, but Cole never moved him because he always liked the way Keith ran the outside unit. But with the way he has taken care of Savannah since she came to the house, Keith is now guaranteed the spot. Cole just hopes he'll take it.

"On your backs," Cole orders. "Sit ups—go."

"Yes, Colonel," the men shout in unison.

Cole glances at Mark, who is on his phone. He is smiling, then quickly hangs up. After a hundred sit ups, Cole orders the men to stand in rows and pick up a long, thick log.

"You lift the log over your head, to your other shoulder and repeat this till I say otherwise," Cole instructs. "Do not move your head. Go."

Cole walks through the rows of men, making sure none of them is slacking on lifting their part of the weight. He stops in front of number thirty-four, who slumps to his knees.

"What's you problem, candidate?" Cole barks.

"Legs aren't working, sir."

"You need to see a medic?"

"No, sir."

"Then get back up and lift that log!" he demands. "You think it's fair for the rest of your team to carry the weight while you take a rest?"

"No, sir."

"Then move!"

The man squeezes his eyes as he tries to stand. He's finished; Cole can see it. "I can't."

"Are you VW?"

"Yes, sir."

"I need to hear you say it."

"I voluntary withdraw."

"Okay, thirty-four, head that way and give your name to Major Paul." He orders the rest of the men to lay the logs down.

Cole moves along the rows. "Drop and roll, candidates." The men drop to the ground and roll all the way to one end of the pit, then roll back. Over and over again. He notices another man slowing down, holding the other men up.

He strolls over to his line. "If seven-eight can't keep up, roll over him," he shouts to the men who are enjoying the holdup. "Seven-eight, are you getting dizzy?"

"No, sir."

"Seven-eight, are you getting tired?"

"No, sir."

"Then why are you holding up your line?"

"Sorry, sir." He picks up his pace just a little. Cole nods to a medic to watch this one for vertigo.

Cole continues down the line of men. "This isn't for the weak, candidates. If you can't make it here, what makes you think you can make it out there?" His voice booms throughout the building. "You're part of a team, and if you forget you are a part of a team, then we will send you home. If you can't follow orders, we will send you home. If you don't pull your own weight, we will send you home. It's all mental, do you understand me?"

"Yes, Colonel!" they all yell out.

"Now on your feet. You have five minutes to get your gear and check the information outside."

"Colonel Logan," Major Paul yells, catching his attention from the men. "You have a visitor." Paul's face gives nothing away but he can probably see a ping of excitement spread through Cole. He nods, signaling for Mark Lopez to take over.

Cole briskly walks over to the main building. The cold air wipes his face, making his eyes sting. His stomach is in his throat as he opens the double doors and heads to the front desk.

"Hi, Colonel," the receptionist greets him. He nods outside with a little wink.

The moment he steps outside his eyes lock on to hers, and everything in his body comes alive. God, he loves this woman. A sexy smile runs across her lips then she breaks out in a full sprint, jumping into his arms and wrapping her legs around his waist.

"Hi, baby." She grins, her eyes sparkling with need.

"Hi." His voice is husky as he grips her body tighter around him. She wiggles, feeling how turned on he is. He's been deprived of her for five days, and he's been hard since he left her that night. He sees Keith grinning behind him before he waves goodbye.

"Is this allowed?" she asks suddenly, looking around at where they are. She tries to free herself from his grip, but he grabs her head, slamming her lips to his, just needing to taste her. She squeaks but gives in, running her hands through his hair and giving it a hard pull. "Cole," she pants, "your room now."

He drops her to the ground, takes her bag in one hand and her hand in the other, and beelines it to his room. Her laughter only makes him pick up the pace.

"Hey, Savi." Mark grins from the stairway, blocking his path to his release.

"Move," Cole grunts. *I need this woman under me now.*

Mark's eyes light up. He fucking knows what he's doing. "So, Savi, how has it been—?"

"Move, Mark." Savannah laughs, shoving him out of the way and leading Cole to his bedroom.

Cole turns over his shoulder. "Cover my next shift."

"Yeah." He chuckles and goes to leave, but not before he calls out, "Don't break any furniture."

"No promises," Savi whispers, stopping at the top of the stairs. She looks up at him and licks her lips. "It's been like a hundred and twenty-three hours since I've seen you. I almost forget what you feel like."

"In that case, let me remind you." Cole unlocks the door and barely has it shut when he grabs her and pushes her up against the wall. His knee is between her legs, holding her in place as he yanks off his shirt and unbuckles his belt. She manages to remove her shirt in record time too. He removes her pants and panties just as she grips his shoulders and jumps up wrapping her legs around his waist.

"I've missed you." She giggles as his grin grows wider.

Shattered

"Let me show you how much I have. Shower with me?" he asks as she nods, running her hands through his hair and giving it a small tug. He growls as he walks them into the bathroom.

She yelps as he places her on the cold counter. "Sorry." He laughs as he tugs his pants off and starts the water.

Her gaze drops to his erection and she lets out a hungry moan. "You can make it up to me."

"I intend to, a few times." He grips the back of her knees and tugs her forward, and his fingers slip inside her easily. "Mmm, you were ready for me." He groans as he pushes his fingers in further, feeling her velvet insides squeeze around him.

"I'm always ready when it comes to you, Cole." She flops her head against his chest. "Please, I need you."

He pulls his hand away and lines himself up with her. He nudges the tip inside, relishing how tight she is.

"Oh, baby," he whispers as he slowly makes his way into her. Yes, this is his Atlantis. He feels her breath blow out across his skin; everything feels so intense when they are like this. So raw and primal.

"Remind me." She wraps her legs around his waist, pulling him deeper. Her hands reach for his dog tags and guide him to her lips.

Cole clutches her waist and lifts her off the counter and steps into the shower. He pulls out and turns her around, pressing her into the wet tile. He grabs his solid erection and spreads her legs to make room for him. He slides back in, pressing his front into her back. He raises her arms above her head, entwining their fingers together. He thrusts forward hard, making her shoot up the tile, and her scream only fuels him further. His hips continue to thrust as he spreads kisses down her neck and shoulders.

"Cole," she moans, leaning her head back on his shoulder. "Yes."

"Who do you belong to, baby?"

"You," she replies without missing a beat. "I belong to you."

"Hell, yeah, you do," he pants as he plows into her. His hands are everywhere; he needs to touch every inch of her. Her little sounds lead him in a path that she desires. "I love you so damn much." This pushes her over the edge. She screams and shakes in his arms, and he comes right afterward, pumping her full of five days' worth of pent-up stress.

She turns to face him and reaches for his neck, her eyes sparkling. "I love you too, Cole, so much it hurts sometimes."

He kisses the tip of her nose before he washes her off and wraps her in a towel then does the same to himself. They lie naked in bed watching the sun slowly set.

"You hungry?" he asks, fingering her damp hair. "Dinner will be served in twenty."

She pushes at his chest, forcing him to lie back, and crawls up on his lap. "That should be enough time for what I have in mind."

Thirty-five minutes later they walk out of his room and down to the dining hall.

***

Savannah

I smile up at him as we walk down the stairs, feeling very satisfied. "I have to admit this uniform is incredibly sexy."

"The green makes my eyes pop," he jokes, making me laugh.

"Are you going to be all scary when you're with the men?"

"Not unless they step out of line." He peers down at me. "This is the last hurdle for making the cut for Green Berets, Savannah. We're here to see if they have what it takes. We yell, but it's nothing they can't handle. A lot of these men have been in the Army for a long time, and those who haven't will learn quickly enough."

"I guess." I sigh, thinking the Army would be no place for me. "So have you found anyone you like yet?"

"A few, but there's one in particular I've been watching."

"Who?"

"Fifty-nine."

"Does he not have a name?"

"Not here, he doesn't. They're all assigned a number so they're all equal."

"Oh." *Makes sense.*

"Ready?" he asks as we approach the door.

"Wait, what if they ask me questions?"

"No one will be asking you questions. You'll be sitting with Blackstone and my father."

"Daniel is here?" I suddenly feel happy. I love

Daniel like he is my own father.

"Yes."

"Wait." I grab his hand. "I don't want to be disrespectful in there, so what do I call you?"

He laughs as he opens the door. "Come on, baby." He places his hand on my lower back and walks me through the door.

I swear the entire place goes silent and all eyes are on me. "You're not in uniform, that's why everyone is staring." *Yeah, that's why…*or maybe it's because the big bad Colonel has a civilian female in the dining hall.

Daniel rises to his feet and wraps me in his usual bear hug. "Good to see you, sweetheart."

"You too." I beam as I take a seat next to Cole.

"You've made quite the stir here." John laughs as the dining hall grows noisy again. "Everyone wants to know who the civilian is with the Colonel."

"I trust you set them right," Cole notes, rather than asks.

"Nah, I figured this way would be more fun," John smirks as he hops to his feet. "Come on, we're up." He nods to the cafeteria line.

"Colonel?" a guy wearing number sixty-one says, standing behind us. "May I have a word with you?"

Cole sighs as he stands. "Savi, go ahead with John and get something to eat. I'll meet you back here."

"All righty, you ready for a five star meal? We have chicken or chicken or chicken." John laughs as he digs in, taking a huge portion of hunter chicken. I take a small amount and pair it with a roll and veggies. "Here." He hands me a bottle of water. "Grab a knife and fork from there," he points to a tray, "and we're done."

"Hang on," a guy, says handing me a napkin. "There you go."

"Thanks." I go to move, but he shifts in front of me.

"Here, let me." He takes my tray out of my grip and starts walking back to the table. It's a nice gesture; if only half the place wasn't watching us. I notice his number is nine, and I think I spot his table because they are the ones who seem most interested. Then it clicks, making me chuckle.

"So what do you win by carrying my tray to the table?" I ask as I come up next to him. He attempts to hide his smile but it doesn't work.

"To be team captain on whichever assignment I choose." He blushes slightly. "When you show leadership, you stick out more. I need to gain as many points here as possible."

I see Cole watching us out of the corner of my eye, and I see our table watching me too. "Tell me something, nine, what's your name?"

He stands a little straighter. "Corporal Davie."

"Do you know who I am?"

"No, miss, I don't."

"Pretty risky for you to take on that bet."

"I like to take risks, but I figured being a gentleman wasn't causing any harm," he shrugs innocently.

"Are you being a gentleman?" I question his motives.

"Yes, miss, I was raised right. My mamma always says you respect a lady and they'll respect you."

I reach for the tray just as Cole does. "Cole," I glance up at him, "Corporal Davie here was kind enough to carry my tray for me. Wasn't that nice?"

Cole studies my face and nods. "Yes, it was. Come on, baby, let's go eat."

I see Davie's eyes pop open when he realizes he just carried the Colonel's girlfriend's tray.

"Thanks again, Davie," I call over my shoulder as I follow Cole back to the seat.

I watch as Davie sits at his table and no one speaks a word. "Cole," I begin, and he turns to look at me. "Has nine been doing well?"

Cole shrugs. "Not overly. He's weak in the water."

"Do you think he'll make the cut?"

"No not unless he gets past his fear of drowning."

I'm confused. "Isn't that a normal fear?"

"Green Berets can't be scared of anything."

I scrunch my face up, trying to follow. "So you're telling me you're scared of nothing."

He wipes his napkin over his mouth then stares down at me with a look that almost frightens me. "Just you."

"Me?"

He leans in a little closer, resting his arm on the back of my chair. "I'm scared to death of losing you." I want to make a comment, but I don't. It wasn't Cole's fault he was taken from me before. Sometimes I have to remind myself of that; a part of me finds it easier to lash out than to accept what really happened.

"You won't lose me, Cole. I love and trust you more than anyone." I see a pained look run across his face. He picks up my left hand and rubs my wedding ring finger. I think he's going to say something, but he doesn't. I reach up and quickly run my hand over his five o'clock shadow. "I wish I knew what this face means." He takes my hand and gives it a quick kiss, then turns his attention back to his dinner.

"Savi," Daniel calls out, "how long you staying at camp?"

"Umm, just until tomorrow afternoon," I answer. "I have a date in the evening."

"Oh?" Cole raises an eyebrow.

"Yes, dinner and a hike." I feel Cole stiffen at the word hike.

"Who's the lucky fellow?" Mark asks through a mouthful of chicken.

"Make that plural. It's with Abby, June, and Sue," I laugh. "There's a meteor shower."

"And?" Cole asks, making me roll my eyes.

"Keith and Mike, possibly Derek, but he was muttering about it being cold when we were out last night. Such a baby," I chuckle until I see Cole's jaw flex. Oops. "We were just walking along the water's edge. The house can be busy sometimes."

"I see." Cole leans back and pushes his plate away. "And where was Keith?"

"Umm…he was dealing with Frank." I notice Cole glances at Mark and then his father. The tension starts to build the more we sit in silence.

"So," I look at everyone, "can I get a tour?"

After the grand tour of the grounds, I can feel Cole stewing about something. He has been off since dinner, and I would bet money on it being that I mentioned spending time alone with Derek. It's quite cold out as we walk back to the main building. I see some of the men heading toward their bunks.

"Are they heated?" I ask.

"Yes, but just enough so they don't get hypothermia."

"Yikes," I whisper.

"Don't have heaters in the mountains, just what's on your back."

"That sucks."

"It always sucks."

"Then why do it?"

He stops at a whiteboard and starts scribbling something.

'03:00 60km Barrel run'

Yikes.

"Personally, I couldn't imagine doing anything else." Cole tilts his head up toward the sky.

I tuck my freezing hands into my jacket. "Even after what…happened?"

His gaze drops to the ground. "I know it's hard to understand, but yes."

A few of the guys are hanging around a large fire pit. We make our way toward them. I wish so much I could hear what's running through Cole's head right now. Something is definitely off.

"Evening, Colonel." One of the candidates nods politely at Cole. "Miss," he says as he addresses me.

So this is fifty-nine, the one Cole has been

Shattered

watching.

"Roth," Cole says. I notice he doesn't address him as his number. Maybe it's because they're not training at the moment. Another man comes up to join us. He is much shorter than Cole and Roth, almost eye level with me.

"Colonel Logan, it's nice to meet you," the man says. "I'm Captain James. I was happy to hear our half of the group got to train here at Camp Green." He looks at me. "So this is the lady who's got the camp buzzing." He extends a hand. "Captain James."

"Nice to meet you, Captain." I shake his hand then quickly shove mine back in my jacket. Cole puts his hand on my waist, moving me in front of him so I am closer to the fire.

Cole and Roth start talking about Roth's time over in Afghanistan. I tune them out, leaning my weight into Cole. His hands are stroking methodically up and down my arms. It feels nice as I watch the fire crackle and pop.

"Lovely girl you got there," I hear Roth say. "Well, I should hit the sack. I see we're going to be up shortly."

"Good night, Roth." Cole leans down, whispering in my ear, "You seem quiet."

"I'm comfy," I answer, still in my trance from the fire. He chuckles as he wraps his arms around me.

"I want to take you to bed."

"And I want you to." I sigh, loving the way I feel in his arms.

***

"MOVE, MOVE, MOVE!" Cole shouts at the men as each one carries his teammate across a field three feet deep in snow.

I see Roth carrying James like he was weightless, taking long strides well ahead of the rest of them.

"If they fall," Daniel says, handing me a coffee, "they have to go back to the start and do it all over again."

"Really?" I ask in disbelief as he takes a seat next to me on the bench.

"Yes, they have to know they can't fail. Most of these men can do it. It's all mental."

We watch as two men fall and don't get back up. Cole goes over and starts yelling at them. I can't make out what he's saying, but it doesn't sound nice. I cringe, feeling bad for the guys.

"He'll ask them what's wrong," Daniel says, noticing I'm shifting uneasily. "See?" He points. "See how Cole nods at someone? That's the medic. He's letting them know that the men are all right, but to keep an eye on them. He'll ask the men if they are VW, voluntary withdrawing. If they are, they will be asked to leave right away." Daniel looks at me. "We are not here to break the men. We are here to make sure we let in America's best. These are all great soldiers. They're just not all great Green Berets."

I watch Cole reach in his pocket and take out his cell phone. He glances over at us and answers the call. After a few minutes he motions for another man to take his place. He signals something to his father, who then excuses himself to follow Cole into the main building.

"Excuse me," I ask one of the men working a stopwatch a while later. "Could you tell me the time?"

"Sure, it's fifteen hundred."

"Three p.m.?"

"Yes." He smiles.

Cole and Daniel have been gone for over an hour and a half, and Keith will be here to pick me up shortly. I decide to go over to the main building, where I run into Davie from the dining hall.

"Hello again," he says, coming up to me sporting a broken nose.

"Oh, ouch!"

"It's fine. At least I got a breather." He shrugs.

"Have you seen Colonel Logan?"

"I did, he's in the main office," he points down the hallway, "second door on your right."

"Thanks, and good luck to you."

"Thanks, I'm gonna need it."

I hear some shouting as I get closer, and I pause outside the door, not sure what I should do. I decide to take a seat next to the door. Ten minutes later the door opens and out walks a woman holding a bunch of files. She's turned away from me and doesn't shut the door all the way as she hurries off in the opposite direction.

"I don't like that idea, son," I hear Daniel say. "I see what you're saying, but it's suicide."

"I know, but if I can get back in under The American's hold, if I can get them to think they've got me—"

What?

"Logan, if they find that wire, they'll kill you on the spot," Mark hisses.

"They won't," Cole argues. "We need that information. We are so close. If we don't do this, Savannah will never be free. Her father knows so much. We can get these fuckers!"

Cole's words echo in my head, as everything else around me goes quiet. I don't even realize I am moving until I'm back up in his room gathering my bag, and I hear Keith's voice.

I slip out of the room and head down the stairs where Cole is quietly chatting with Keith in the corner. He stops and plasters on a smile when he sees me coming. *I'm tired of all this whispering.*

"Hey, baby, sorry about leaving you right before you have to go."

"Is everything all right?" My voice sounds off, and I know he hears it too. His eyes narrow as he studies my face.

"Yes, of course." He leans in and gives me a kiss. I try to respond, but I am in too much shock with what I just heard to act normal. This is not the time to talk about it with him, though. "Hey, are *you* all right?"

"Mmmhmm." I glance at Keith, seeing his face is stressed. "I'll see you in a few days, right?"

"Yes, of course." He leans down once more and kisses me. I want to ask him to promise me, but I know he'd ask start asking more questions. "I love you."

"I love you too."

Shattered

The trip home is uneventful, and after everything is unpacked, I head for the kitchen where I run into Derek, who is in a foul mood.

"Savi, could you ask Mike to meet me in the garage? He's in Cole's office."

"Sure, Derek." I smile, not wanting to know what is pissing him off right now.

I knock on the door and see Mike on the phone. "Derek needs you in the garage."

"Okay, thanks." He rushes past me. "Shit, could you give that file on the desk to Keith?"

"Sure, no problem."

"Thanks!"

I move over to Cole's desk and pick up the file. As I do, some papers fall out and land on the other side of the desk. I start picking them up, when I glance at the computer and see a forwarded email to Cole from Frank with my father's name as the subject.

I have never invaded someone's privacy before, but this e-mail involves me, and I'm tired of not knowing anything.

I strain to listen for any voices, but all is quiet. I shift and click on the email but stay on my knees, hidden in case anyone comes in. I don't want to run the risk having anyone catch me, so I press print and wait till the two pages came out. I fold and tuck the papers into my back pocket. I collect the file for Keith and click out of the e-mail back to the inbox.

Once I finally get a moment alone in my room, I pull out the papers. I take a deep breath and scan the email.

Logan, how would you like us to deal with this?

Holy shit!

My father is reaching out to Frank about knowing I am alive and being protected by the U.S. Army in a safe house somewhere in the States. He's not angry they've had me for so long without telling him. He just wants to see me. *Wants to hold his daughter he thought was dead.* Tears slip down my face as I read. My father pours his heart out to Frank, begging him to let him see me.

I read Cole's reply.

Frank, I just did. See below.

My eyes scan his words back to my father. I'm confused. Why is Cole telling him that he doesn't deserve to see me? There are answers to be had before he will *ever* let him see me.

My back hits the wall then my butt sinks to the ground, hard. Things don't make sense. Why would my father reach out to Frank? How did he find out I was here? Why hasn't Cole told me about the email? And why would Cole want to risk his life to get answers from The American?

After a long time on the floor, I finally stand. I know what I need to do.

Later, I try to act normal with everyone up on the hill, but I can feel Keith watching me. I know he knows something is bothering me. He tried to pry it out of me on the drive home, but I was too blown away by Cole's idea about letting himself be taken by The American again to let him get it out of me.

Derek is my target tonight. He has a weak spot for me, and I intend to use it. I wait for the meteor shower to start, then slowly make my way over to where Derek is standing.

Shattered

"Pretty neat, huh?" Derek whispers, as little bursts of light travel across the sky. "Amazing to think they're two million years old."

Here it goes.

"Derek, I have a problem." His gaze drops to mine. "And I think only you can help me."

"Oh?"

"Can we speak privately?"

He studies my face, seeing I am indeed struggling with something, then glances over at Keith. "Savi needs to go back to the house."

"I can take her," Keith says, rising out of his chair.

"It's cool. I'll take her. I need to use the bathroom anyway." Keith's eyes narrow on me again, so I muster up a smile and shrug.

Derek leads the way down the path as I follow behind, sorting what I want to ask in my mind. I stop him at the stairs, not wanting to go inside. I don't trust anyone overhearing, and knowing the guys can lip read off the cameras, I am even more cautious.

Derek leans against the railing and tucks his gloved hands into his coat pockets. "What's going on, Savannah?"

I rub my mitts together more out of nerves than the cold. "I know you and Cole have a stressful past, but I also know that when it comes down to it you would be there to help him out, right?"

He shrugs. "Yeah, I guess."

"What if I told you I know something bad is going to happen to Cole, and only I could stop it? Would you help me?"

He rubs his chin, sensing he's not going to like what I have to say. "I'm listening."

"I came across something that wasn't intended for my eyes, but…whatever, I read it."

"Ah, shit," he sighs, "what was it?"

"An email from my father to Frank. He wants to see me." Derek stops moving. "Cole emailed him back, saying that the only way he'd let my father see me again is if he got some answers." I pause and glance up at him. "Derek, I can get these answers. I think my father is being blackmailed by the people who kidnapped me. I need to see him and help him. We haven't always had the greatest relationship, but he's still my father. I need you to fly me to New York and get me to him."

Derek's face is unreadable. His gaze drops to the ground then he leans back, rests against the railing, and lets out a long breath. I hold my breath and wait, but he takes too long. So I decide to try my other concern, *one* thing Agent York and I did agree on. "I'm scared that if we don't fix this soon, they might come after the house. Cole is planning on getting himself taken by The American again." I step closer to Derek. "You of all people saw what happened to me while he was gone. I can't let that happen again. So you either help me, or I'll figure it out my way."

He shakes his head. "Why haven't you gone to Cole about this?"

"Seriously?" I roll my eyes. "Have you met Cole?"

A tiny smirk graces his face. "Point taken. I'm sure if he could wrap you in bubble wrap, he would."

"I'm thinking more a foam padded room."

Derek starts to pace in front of me. I can picture the wheels turning in his head.

"You know he will have me fired for helping you."

"I won't let that happen, you have my word." I try to hide my smile. "Are you saying you'll help me?"

"You haven't left me a choice, have you? I say yes and get you there and back safely, or I say no and you leave and get yourself in a shit load of trouble. Either way, I'm fucked."

I sag with relief. "Thank you, truly, Derek."

"Fuck," he hisses under his breath, "why couldn't you have asked Keith?"

"He would have said no, and tied me to the chair till Cole comes home."

"Smart man." He starts walking down the porch stairs. "Come on, we should get back. I'll make some calls tonight. Be ready to leave for 'town' tomorrow morning. Leave your bag packed inside your bedroom. I'll grab it on my way downstairs, and we'll head out from there."

"All right," I nod. "Thank you again, Derek. I knew I could count on you," I say, feeling my stomach twist into a painful knot. I don't want to lie to Cole, and I certainly don't want to leave him, but I will not stand by while he gives himself over to The American. This ends now.

***

I fold the letter and place it on Cole's pillow, knowing I'll get a few days' head start before he sees it. Hopefully Keith will not want to tag along today. Poor Keith. I know he'll be upset, but hopefully in time he'll understand too.

I fling my purse over my arm and head downstairs.

"Good morning," Abigail says, handing me a cup of coffee. "I never got to ask you, how was your visit with Cole at Camp Green?"

I slide onto the stool, wondering where Derek is. "It was really nice to see him. After seeing what he does there, you can bet I'll never cut it as a Green Beret."

"Ha! Me either, dear." She laughs, cracking two eggs into the frying pan.

She starts talking as I hear a hissing sound off to my left and see Derek, waving for me to follow.

He mouths, "Time to go."

I feel uneasy as I get to my feet. I would be lying if I said I wasn't terrified about leaving the grounds…leaving this town without Cole. Wrapping my arms around Abigail from behind, I give her a big hug.

"I love you, Abigail."

"Oh, sweetie," she coos, covering my hands with hers, "I love you too."

I don't let go, and hold on an extra minute. "Please know I wouldn't be who and where I am today if it wasn't for you."

She turns to look at me, but I back away, ducking my head. "I'll be back later."

I think she thinks I don't want her to see I'm

Shattered

emotional, because she lets me leave without another word.

I'm almost to the door before Keith calls out my name. *Damn, almost made it!* I suck in a sharp breath and turn to look up at him as he trots up to me.

"Hey, I was wondering if you'd like to come with me to pick up Cole later on in the week. He'd love it."

I feel my friggin' eyes betray me as they go glossy. "Yeah, sure…that sounds, um, like a good plan."

"Hey." He comes closer, tilting his head to the side. I feel his eyes penetrating my defenses. This guy is good. "Everything all right?"

"Oh, yeah." I hate to use this, and I'm sure as shit going to go to hell for saying it. "Just having a down day." I shrug, alluding to my miscarriage, but to be truthful there hasn't been a day I don't think about our little something who could have been. *Ahh…not now, Savannah!*

Keith's face drops as he studies my face carefully. "Cole warned me, but I truly didn't see it until now."

"What? What are you talking about?" I'm thrown by his comment.

His lips press together as he once again studies my face long and hard. I can almost feel his eyes burning into my brain, probing the part that's holding my lie at bay.

"Anything you want to tell me, Savannah?" His voice is low.

I swallow hard, feeling my forehead break out in

a line of sweat. "No."

Yeah, that was convincing…

Feeling terribly guilty, I slowly walk away from him, but I stop and turn to look back, chewing on the inside of my lip while my brain struggles to find the right words.

"Keith?"

"Yes?"

"Thank you."

"For what?"

I shrug attempting to play it cool. "Just—for everything."

He takes a step toward me as I take one back. "Savannah—"

"Savi, you ready?" Derek asks, coming into the entryway. "I need to be at Christine's in an hour, so I gotta go." He nods at Keith. "Hey, man, we're heading to town. You need anything?"

"No," he shakes his head, his eyes still on me. "I'm good."

"Talk to you later, Keith," I mumble.

"I hope so," I hear him say as I close the door.

Chapter Five

The drive to town is painful. My hands are twisted on my lap as we come to the town's outer limits. My legs are jittery, my heart's trying to escape the growing anxiety, and all the while I'm blinking away tears for Cole.

"We'll park and transfer into Agent Stall's car. He'll drive us to the airport," Derek announces while we wait at a stoplight. He glances at me. "Now is the time if you're having second thoughts, Savannah."

"No," I squeeze out, and watch as the stoplight turns to green. Little snowflakes dust the windshield, making me shiver. I hope I'm doing the right thing. I'm past changing my mind now, as I know I must prevent Cole from putting himself in danger in order to help me again.

Agent Stall is not overly friendly. He barely says two words the whole three-hour drive to the airport. I am handed an ID with the name Nicole Johnson and a printout of my airline ticket. We quickly board, taking our seats toward the front of the plane.

It isn't first class, but executive...not bad. I notice Derek needs the extra leg space. He stretches out, then pushes the call button and asks the flight attendant for an orange juice. He seems relaxed.

I, on the other hand, am having an internal anxiety attack. So many things are blowing through my brain. I'm terrified of the answers I'm headed toward.

Once we are up in the air and the seat belt sign is turned off, I hop up, nearly plowing over Derek to get to the bathroom. Inside the tiny room I lean over the sink and splash cold water over my face. "*I can do this. I can do this. I can do this.*" I close the lid to the toilet, take a seat, and run my hands through my hair. "Calm down, Savi." I try to remember Dr. Roberts and his relaxing techniques...in through the nose, out through the mouth, count to thirty, breathe slowly again...then rubbing my sweaty hands over my jeans, I take a moment to think.

A loud knock makes me jump to my feet. Opening the door, I'm faced with an annoyed woman who eyes me with obvious hostility.

"Only two bathrooms for sixty passengers," she mumbles as she shoves her son in ahead of her.

"Sorry," I whisper, although I'm not. I'm sure she'd prefer me to freak out in the bathroom than in front of everyone, including her child. Rude woman.

"You okay?" Derek asks once I return to my seat and fumble with the belt.

"Sure." I lean my head back and close my eyes.

Luckily, the layover in Salt Lake City is only thirty minutes, just enough time to find our gate and grab a coffee.

Four hours into the flight, I feel the plane start its descent. I clench the arm rests until my fingers turn white. Derek takes pity on me and attempts to distract me.

"Okay, so once we land, a friend of mine will meet us at baggage. From there we'll go right to your father's office. I have eyes on him currently, so if he leaves we will find where he is and change route."

"We're going there today?" The words fall off my tongue.

Derek turns in his seat to look at me straight on. "Savannah, we have a flight to catch tomorrow night. You have this one chance to get your information. I'm already putting you in danger by taking you off the Shadow grounds." He rubs his face. "I'm seriously going to be stripped of my job for this."

"Then why are you helping me?" I ask, needing to know.

He turns to face forward again, downing his juice and crushing the cup under his hand. "I have my reasons."

"Which are?" I ask, being nosy, but I need the distraction, and honestly I want to know.

He clears his throat and shoves the crushed cup into the pouch hanging off the wall. "I fucked up when I was on the team. I was young and dumb." He shrugs, but I can see what he did weighs on him. "So maybe this will show them I can be trusted, that I can get you back safely, and with answers." He lets out a laugh. "Or maybe not, since this is insane."

The captain's voice blares over the speakers, announcing our arrival. Jeez, I hadn't noticed we landed.

"If it means anything, Derek, thank you."

"Yeah, sure thing." He looks out the window, and I know our heart to heart is over.

***

Cole

Cole goes over his checklist, finding what time fifty-nine is scheduled to complete the blind navigation course in the woods. The candidates have to navigate through the woods with only a map. If they're caught using their head lamp, they get a point taken off. It's no surprise fifty-nine, Adam Roth, is at the head of the pack.

Since he is so close to finishing, Cole decides to meet Roth at the last checkpoint to talk to him about the possibility of joining the house. He's on his way when he spots Keith pulling up to the main house. It's dark, but he can see there's something wrong when the other man jumps quickly from the car.

"Keith?" Cole shouts. Keith stops, then turns and begins to head in his direction.

Cole sees his father coming out of the main building to join them. Obviously his father knows something isn't right either.

"What are you doing here?" Cole asks, once he's close enough.

Keith points at the main office. "Let's talk

inside."

Mark joins them as well. Keith clears his throat, looking pale and sweaty.

"Where are John and Paul?" he asks, seeming to gather himself.

"They're still out in the field. What's going on?" Cole asks between clenched teeth.

"I don't have all the details yet, but Derek took Savannah to town this morning and they haven't returned."

Cole's stomach drops as his head tries to process what was just said.

"What do you mean?" Daniel asks, crossing his arms. "Did you trace the SUV? They all have trackers, you know that."

"I did, and it was parked outside Christina's store. We checked, of course, and she said they didn't come in but figured they were planning to after they did some errands. She didn't think about it till later, as she got busy. She did remember seeing a black truck drive by a couple of times. I got the plate number, and it's registered to an Agent Michael Stall."

"Did you get hold of Stall?" Mark asks, shaking his head.

Cole's hands ball into fists at his sides—something's off. Derek is an ass, but he wouldn't hurt Savi.

"Yes, and after some threatening, it turns out Derek paid him to drive him and Savannah to the airport."

"Airport?" Mark hisses, glancing at Cole. "Why the fucking airport?"

Keith glances at Cole and lets out a long breath. "I have a theory." All eyes turn to Keith as he continues. "This morning Savannah was acting really strange. Abigail said Savannah was acting almost like she was saying goodbye. She did the same to me. I could tell she was lying about something. She's a bad liar." He pulls out a piece of paper from his back pocket. "I found this in her wastebasket in her room." He hands it to Cole.

Cole quickly unfolds it and scans the words. *Fuck!*

"What is it?" Mark moves to his side, trying to read the paper.

"She found the email from her father to Frank, and my reply." Cole's words are quiet. "Dad," he looks to Daniel and feels all the blood rush from his face, "she's walking into a trap."

Cole,

I came to this house stripped of everything, and you built me into something. I have never felt whole, never felt a sense of belonging, never felt true love until I met you.

My leaving is to give you something you gave me—peace. There are so many lies that surround me. They need to be dealt with, and only I can find the answers. I'm tired of being broken. I'm ready to fix this. I will not let you hurt for me again. I know I can do this and I'll soon be back in your arms.

You will forever be my knight who stormed the castle wall and saved me from all the evil that held me prisoner.
I love you, Cole Logan.
Forever yours,
Savannah x

Cole sits on the edge of the bed, his hands shaking as he re-reads her letter for the tenth time, fighting back the nausea that's pooling in the back of his throat.

"Oh, baby, you just walked into the lion's den," he mutters as he picks up his duffel bag.

"Ready when you are," Mark calls out softly from the doorway.

***

Savannah

I watch the familiar scenery fly by. As we ride in the tinted Ford Explorer to my father's office, my mind wanders. Well, I've wanted to know what this would feel like ever since I was taken to my own personal hell almost ten months ago. It doesn't feel like home anymore; it feels cold and crowded. I suddenly miss the wide open space of the Montana mountains, my friends, and yes, my family. New York City isn't right for me anymore. I have found peace and happiness—I've moved on.

The weight in my belly that's been forming since I stepped on the plane is getting heavier as we drive closer to the office. My fingers catch and run along the chain to the tiny snowflake that hasn't left my neck since Cole gave it to me. I'm so nervous my leg is bouncing wildly, making a thumping noise on the floor.

Derek's phone rings, and I flinch. I watch his face when he reads the caller ID. He swallows hard as he answers the call.

"Logan."

I hold my breath and watch Derek's eyes squeeze shut.

"Yeah, one second." He looks at me and holds out the phone. I don't want to take it, I can't, but…

"Cole?" My voice gives away how much I miss him.

"Savannah," the worry is thick in his voice, "what the hell are you doing?"

"Ending this."

"It's not the way!" he nearly shouts.

My anger surfaces. "Right, and you getting taken by The American again is?"

Silence.

"I heard you talking at the camp, Cole. I can't go through that again. It's time I finish this. I love you more than anyone or anything, so it's time I get the answers. I deserve it, but without anyone else putting themselves in danger for me." He attempts to say something, but I cut him off. "I'll be all right. I'm just going to figure out who's blackmailing my father so I can find out who is actually behind my kidnapping."

"No, Savannah, you don't—"

"I'll be home tomorrow night. I love you Cole."

I quickly hang up, turn off the phone, and hand it back to Derek, who is wide-eyed.

"Problem?" I ask, feeling a new sense of strength. I knew I could do this. I have to do this, for Cole and me to move on with our lives.

"Not at all." Derek smirks briefly and goes back to looking out the window.

***

"Here." Derek gives me a tiny cell phone that fits inside a small pocket in my dress. It looks like a remote I had for the Apple TV back in my old life. "Just in case we get separated, speed dial one is me, and two is Cole. You don't have to look, just feel where the buttons are."

I nod and feel for the little buttons until I am familiar with how to press them. I'm still not sure what the hell I'm going to say when I see my father.

We are in a café across the road from my father's office building. I've changed into a black Ponte sheath dress with heels and stockings. I have to look like I belong in the corporate world so Derek and I can walk in and not stand out. Derek's connections got us in contact with a woman on the tenth floor. She's going to meet us downstairs and walk us in so we don't have to give a name to the front desk, and then we can bypass security. We don't want anyone knowing I'm here.

"Put these on." Derek hands me a pair of thick-rimmed glasses. I do, as Derek shrugs on a trench coat over his dark blue suit and then he helps me into mine.

"Ready?" he asks.

"Yeah...yes, I am." I try to produce a brave a smile, but I'm a mixture of fear and, strangely, excitement.

We step outside, letting the freezing New York air swirl around us. Derek links arms with me and helps keep me from slipping on the black ice as we cross the street.

A woman with a friendly smile greets us at the door and speaks to us like we were old friends. Security eyes us but says nothing as the woman puts on a good show for them. I keep my head down, and my scarf wraps around most of my face. As soon as we step into the elevators, Derek thanks the woman and hands her an envelope. Hush money.

People shuffle in and out as we rise through the building. Finally we reach the tenth floor and she turns and leans up to my ear. I stiffen at her closeness and notice Derek reaches for something, but then stops when he sees she's just whispering.

"October TMZ, top left corner. You're not the only one making it in the media." She gives my arm a small squeeze and disappears out the elevator doors.

I'm confused by her comment, but I memorize what she said so I can deal with it later. Derek looks at me, puzzled, and I shake my head, needing to prepare myself for what is ahead. Besides, we don't have time to talk, as the doors soon open to the twenty-sixth floor.

Oh shit.

As much as I'm bundled up, I am cold, and I feel the hairs rise on my arms. Derek and I stop to see if

Shattered

Luka is in his office. His door is closed, so my guess is he is in a meeting. We move on, and before I can think, Derek opens my father's office door.

"Mayor Fox?" Derek says in a direct voice.

My father's grey eyes look up and lock with mine.

Holy...

Chapter Six

Dad.

He blinks a few times before he stands, rounds his desk, and stops a few feet from us. I hear rather than see Derek shift my way.

"Savannah?" my father whispers in disbelief. His face is white as a sheet. "Is that really you?"

"Hi, Dad." I feel the words catch in my throat.

His hands outstretched, he makes his way toward me but hesitates as he comes in for a hug. As soon as his arms are around me I feel…uncomfortable? Weird? Strange? I don't know, but I don't like it.

"I can't believe you're alive." He pulls back and grasps my shoulders. "Look at you."

"Dad, we need to talk, and I don't have much time."

He looks over at the door. "Did anyone see you? Do you think you were followed?"

"No, it's okay. I have some questions that need answers, Dad. Like who's blackmailing you? Do you know why I was taken? Why was my ransom so low?"

Shattered

"Whoa, slow down, dear." He smiles at me, still with his hand on my shoulder. He thinks for a moment, then says, "Tell you what, we need a proper place to talk about all this. Meet me for an early dinner this evening." He smiles at Derek. "Both of you. Come to the house so we can talk without worrying that the media or anyone else will see you. I'll answer your questions then, but not here. It's not safe. You really should go." He suddenly looks uneasy and makes a show about looking over his shoulder.

I glance at Derek, who doesn't like the idea and is obvious about it, but he takes his cue from me and agrees unhappily. "Umm, yeah, okay."

"Great, four sound all right?" Dad asks, as I check the time. It's a little after one. "I'll call ahead and have dinner ready for us."

"All right, we'll meet you there."

My father turns to Derek. "Thank you for bringing her here." He extends his hand for a shake. Derek takes it quickly and moves toward the door.

"Savi." Derek flicks his head for me to follow.

"See you at four, Dad."

"All right, dear." He kisses my forehead. "Be careful. I love you, sweetheart." He sounds so sincere my earlier uneasy feelings evaporate. Wow…it's been a long time since my father uttered those words to me and meant them. There's no media here to make a show for.

"Me too."

"Are you out of your mind?" Derek explodes as soon as we make our way across the street. "That guy is as fake as a three dollar bill, Savi. What are we doing letting him call the shots here? Why—"

I cut him off. "Derek, it's okay. We have no choice. My father was right; his office in broad daylight isn't the right time." Giving him a look, I walk away from him, my own thoughts in a jumble. It was such a shock seeing him again. I need time to process all this myself, and Derek doesn't know my father and how complicated it is being in his position in the Mayor's office.

Derek starts making calls out on the patio as soon as we arrive at our hotel. Derek chose this hotel because it is so close to my father's home. I stare out the window, seeing his penthouse condo across the street with its dark gray curtains. I always thought they were so heavy and dreary for the room, but he insisted on keeping them.

I shower and change into pants and a cream colored blouse. I curl my hair and add earrings and a few bangles to my outfit. I may have been gone for some time, but I know my father will still expect me to dress appropriately, and I will not disappoint.

"Yes, honey, I'll see you soon. I love you too." Derek speaks quietly with his back to me.

I pick up my purse and slip the tiny phone into my bra. I didn't know Derek was seeing someone. He must have noticed the look on my face, because he smiles and rolls his eyes.

"She's the prettiest brown-eyed girl I've ever met." He laughs. "And now she's begging me to bring her home a souvenir from New York."

"Oh, really?" I grin. "You should stop by Draped in Lace. They have—"

His hands fly over his ears, cringing. "That's not

Shattered

something I want to buy my six year old niece!"

"Oh!" I laugh. "In that case, the gift shop downstairs may have something."

"That's where we're headed. I need your help."

After twenty minutes of looking at every knick-knack the gift shop owns, Derek finally decides on a snow globe of the Rockefeller Center ice skating rink at Christmas. It makes a beautiful gift any six year old girl would love. I know because I have...had one.

Convincing him to stop for coffee, we take a seat near the back and enjoy a few minutes before we have to leave. My nose scrunches at Derek's strong black coffee as I blow the steam off the top of mine, adding a little more cream and sugar.

"My parents brought me to New York when I was eleven," he says, breaking our silence. "My sister and I were so excited to see the Rangers play the Kings. That's when Gretsky was playing for them. My parents planned this whole day of fun for us, batting cages in the morning, lunch at Times Square, then the game and ice cream afterward." He smiles, remembering. "Man that was a good trip."

"I bet." I sip my coffee, happy we're talking about anything else but the real reason we're here. "Where are you from originally?"

"Washington, born and raised," he says proudly.

"Are your parents still there?"

His face falls a little. "My old man died a few years back, heart attack. My mom is there, though, with my sister and my niece. My sister left her husband around the same time Dad died, so she moved in with Mom." He pauses. "I try to step up when I can, so my niece has at least some sort of male figure in her life." He glances at me. "Sounds like Frank is moving me back to Washington, which is good because I was planning on transferring anyway. Shadows and me," he shakes his head, "well, let's just say we *ain't* a good mix."

I feel sad, as I do like Derek. He's been a friend, but it's obvious for whatever reason the guys don't like him, and I understand that. Trust goes hand in hand with everything in their line of work.

"Oh, Derek, I hope you'll be happy there." I didn't say Cole had already told me.

He grants me a smile. "I'll miss a few things." He winks.

"Mmm." I chuckle, finishing off my coffee.

"Let's go back up to the room," Derek mumbles, as he checks his phone for the hundredth time. I know he'll be glad to get this over with.

It takes him two times to open the hotel door with the key card. I pretend not to notice, but I can see he's jumpy.

"You all right?" I ask as he pulls down the handle to open the door.

"Yes *I* am," he mutters, letting me walk in first.

Two steps past the threshold, I'm met with a set of intense dark eyes that steals every last ounce of air from my body.

Oh...

We stand two feet apart staring at one another. My heart pounds loudly as he flexes his jaw dramatically for me to see. Instead of feeling nervous, I feel the inner pull that he brings out in me. My tongue darts out and does a swipe along my lower lip. His eyes narrow and I see that familiar flicker. He feels it too, I can tell, but I need to stay strong if I am going to do this. I draw in a deep breath.

"Cole." My voice comes out raspy.

"Savannah." He says each syllable slowly.

"And...I'm gonna leave now," Derek whispers backing out of the hotel room. Neither of us talks until we hear the door close.

"When did you get here?" I ask, turning my back to him and calmly placing my purse on the bar top.

Suddenly both of his arms trap me and his mouth is at my ear. "I'm so angry at you right now...!" *He is actually vibrating.*

"Cole—" He bites at my neck, giving my nerves another jolt.

"Do you have any idea how scared I've been these last twelve hours?" he hisses as runs his hand along my stomach. "I want to handcuff you to me right now and drag your ass back to Montana." His other hand grabs my ass, squeezing it and making my hand drop back against his shoulder. "Why didn't you tell me?"

I close my eyes as his hand slides in the front of my pants, running just shy of where I want him to be. "Because you would have said no."

He whips me around, grabs my waist, and hoists me onto the bar top. He moves between my legs and clutches my lower back, hauling me into him. "Damn right, I would have. You're mine, and I protect what's mine." He reaches over, clasping my chin, and gives me a rough but sensual kiss. By the time he pulls away I'm nearly panting with built-up lust. "Christ, Savannah, are you out of your mind? What if something happened to you? Then what?"

My mind scrambles to think clearly. "Cole, I'm fine. I'm meeting my father to get some answers."

I feel his hands pull away from me, and he runs them roughly through his hair. He closes his eyes, muttering something to himself I can't make out.

"Logan, we have eyes on the building, and we're not the only ones." Mark stands in the doorway. "Hi, Savi." He smiles, raising one eyebrow, but his cheeky smile fades fast when he takes in Cole's expression. *Of course Mark is here.*

"Which building? And who else is here?" I ask, looking from Mark to Cole.

"How many?" Cole's voice is all business.

"Three."

"Will someone answer me?" I try again. "Cole?"

Cole sighs as he thinks. "All right, double our men on theirs and have the snipers ready on my command."

"Snipers?" I nearly shout. "What the hell is going on?" I can tell I'm not going to get anywhere with these two, so I quickly shift off the bar before Cole knows what I'm doing. I grab my purse and head for the front door.

"Where are you going?" Cole calls out to me, signaling for Mark to block the doorway.

I turn on my heel and find him right in front of me. "I'm sick and tired of people not answering me, Cole. Ask your *man* to move! I'm going to talk with Derek. At least *he* acknowledges me when I speak." I eye up where Mark's foot is, ready to stamp on it.

Yeah, I can tell he doesn't like that comment, but

right now I don't care. I feel like I am treading water with no end in sight. Everyone knows things but me, and it's infuriating. I spent seven months with no control over my life, not knowing from one minute to the next what would happen to me, and I will not live like that again. I turn and stare Cole down, because at this moment I am friggin' angry, and I want answers.

Cole looks at me for a moment, his expression tight. "All right, Savi, hold on. As much as I'm against this—you meeting your father this evening—Frank felt it was about time we got some answers, and maybe this is the way to do it." His jaw twitches. *Oh boy, he is mad.* "So, you and *Derek* will attend your father's dinner, but with a wire and plenty of backup." It's not lost on me the way he says Derek's name like it's acid on his tongue.

"Wire?" I swallow. "Isn't that a bit extreme?"

"Extreme?" he shouts, his hands flying to his hips. "Extreme is you running off to New York with *Derek Rent* to confront your father with the Cartel hot on your trail! Extreme is you not seeing what's going on here!"

"The Cartel knows I'm here?"

"When will you get it, Savannah? They have eyes everywhere!"

"Christ, Cole, fill me in, then!" I shout, taking a step toward him. "Please, for once in my goddamn life, will someone tell me something? I'm tired of living in the shadows, only seeing the grey and black!" I take another step until I am right in front of him. "Don't I deserve that much?"

"You deserve the world, Savi." His whisper catches me off guard. I shake my head and try to remain on track.

"Don't be sweet right now, Cole." I pause. "Please," I lower my voice, "don't try to steer me off course. My father did all the time."

"I wasn't trying to." His hands slip around my waist, pulling me in. "It just came out. It's how I feel, and when all of this is over I intend to give it to you." His voice is low but still harsh. I can hear his frustration. "Look, baby, there *are* some things you need to know that are going to—"

"Logan," Mark says. I forgot he's still here. "We need to prep Savannah." He opens the door further, and in walks Keith.

Oh, fuck me!

"How mad is he?" I whisper to Cole.

"Let's just say not as mad as me."

"I am sorry, Cole."

"Let's just get through this." He kisses the top of my head and turns me around to face Keith.

Keith is holding a small box. He stops in front of me and speaks quickly, not looking directly at my face. "This is your tracking device." He opens the box and reveals a silver bracelet with a white stone in the middle. "It's undetectable." He quickly snaps it around my wrist. "Don't," his eyes finally meet mine, and they are cold, "take it off."

"I won't."

"This is the wire." He opens a second box from his pocket and shows me a matching necklace. "This will help—"

My stomach sinks. "I don't want to wear that."

Shattered

My voice caught in my throat.

"You have to," Keith states firmly, but as he looks at me, I can see he has conflicting expressions playing over his face.

I clasp my snowflake pendant. "No, Keith, I haven't taken this off since—" My eyes sting. It represents more than just Cole; it's a little reminder of our baby too.

"Savi," Cole whispers in my ear behind me, "just for the evening. I'll hold on to it and keep it safe." I hold myself very still for a moment then nod, not wanting to speak in fear I'd cry. Cole moves my hair aside. I feel his warm hands move over my skin as he unclasps it. He reaches for the necklace Keith is holding and secures it in place. It feels heavy. I don't like it.

"Testing, testing, one-two-three." Keith says in a quiet voice. John pops his head in the door giving a thumbs up.

Is Paul here too?

"No mention of the house, no mention of any of the guys being here, no mention what you've been up to. Most importantly, don't let them separate you from Derek." Keith warns, "If anything happens and you need us, your safe word is what?"

"Blackstone," I answer without missing a beat.

"Right."

"Guys. I'm going to be all right. It's my father who's in trouble now." I notice Keith glance at Cole. "Now what?"

"We leave in two minutes," Keith says as he turns around.

"Keith," I call out, making him stop. "I didn't

run. I took someone with me and left a note. I was only trying to do the right thing, and I knew you and the rest of the house would never have let me come. Derek was my only chance to make things right."

He turns fully to study me. "I know you were doing what you thought was right. I know you found out what Cole planned to do, so the fact that you wanted to protect him and all of us makes me understand why you did what you did." He pauses. "But that doesn't mean I'm not furious with you, and it doesn't mean I'm not sticking a tracking device on your goddamn ass when we get home." I see his eyes crinkle slightly.

"Deal." I walk over and give him a hard hug. "I love you, Keith. You're family. Thank you for understanding."

"Yeah, well, don't get used to it. I'm not normally, so take what you can get." He gives me a little shove and nods at Cole. "I'll meet you outside the door."

I let out a long breath and try to absorb this situation.

"You ready?" Cole moves in front of me.

"Cole, is there anything I should know before I go in there? Please don't lie to me."

He rubs his chin, thinking. "Know I love you and will do anything to protect you, and when this is all over I intend to make you smile for the rest of your life."

I roll my eyes. "That would have been incredibly romantic if you didn't say it like I was going to war."

"In some ways you are."

Shattered

"What does that even—?"

He grips the sides of my face and kisses me with so much lust I nearly forget what I was about to do. I put my hands on his shoulders as I press myself into his solid body. As quickly as he came in for the kiss, he pulls away and takes my hand.

"I love you." He pulls me toward the door.

"I love you too."

***

Cole

Cole pulls her into the adjoining room where Paul is at the table testing out the pin camera.

"Hey, Savi." Paul gives a tight smile and holds up the pin that is shaped like the New York state flag. "This will be our eyes."

Cole takes the small pin from Paul's fingers and pins it to Savannah's blouse and waves his hand in front of it.

"All good," Paul states.

"Ummm," Savannah is biting her lip. "This is all a bit much."

"No," Cole answers simply, "it's frankly not enough."

"Okay, Savi." Derek enters from the hallway. "You ready to go?"

Cole's eyes narrow in on him. He is still furious at Derek and knows they will be having plenty of words after this is over. His instincts were right when it came to Derek Rent. He still doesn't trust him, and he hates that he still has to use him at all.

"You keep her safe, Rent," he says, pushing his finger hard into his chest, "or I'll personally take you out."

"Cole," Savannah hisses, squeezing her body in the space between them. "Please, let's just go before they decide to put any more devices on me." She turns to look at Cole, trying to act brave, but he can see she's scared. He wants nothing more than to take her home and lock her away in his bedroom and keep her safe from everything. "I'll see you soon." She kisses him on the lips softly, but he swipes his tongue inward, tasting as much of her as he can. She squeaks, making him kiss her harder. Finally he pulls away and lets her catch her breath. "Cole?"

"Yeah?"

"You're going to have to let go." She glances down at his cast-iron grip on her hips.

"Right." He steps back, watching Derek walk her out and unknowingly into the lion's den.

"I don't get it," Keith says, appearing at his side. "I know *we* are under orders not to tell her anything, but are *you* really going to let her go in blind?"

"I know Savannah, Keith. If she goes in knowing who is behind all this, she'll charge them like a pissed off bull. It's safer for her to be her normal innocent self. They'll be less apt to harm her if she truly doesn't know anything."

Keith huffs. "I sure saw it before she left. I should've gone with my gut and followed her."

"No," Cole shakes his head, "you did the right thing and we were able to catch up with them."

"Perhaps, but she's sure as shit not known for

her lying skills."

"Certainly not, and I love that about her," Cole admits.

"Me too."

Suddenly they both feel their conversation is getting awkward, and they start moving about. "Right, well, let's get this over with." Cole sits down at the table, watching the computer monitor.

"Well, fuck me," Mark hisses from the window, staring down at the street a pair of binoculars glued to his eyes. "Logan, you'll never guess who's here."

***

Savannah

I walk nervously down the sidewalk, my arm looped through Derek's, on the way to meet my father. It is starting to snow. I try to act normal, I really do, but after being surprised by Cole and the guys and being lit up like a Christmas tree with trackers, mics, and video equipment, I feel a nervous dance going on in my stomach.

"Maddison, my niece," Derek starts, "she reminds me so much of my sister. She has these big brown eyes like the cat from Puss in Boots." He laughs. "All that little girl has to do is look up at me and I turn all mushy. I'm visiting her after we get back home, and I'm going to take her to Disney World. She loves Sleep In Beauty. I've ordered her that princess dress from the movie. I'm soon to be her favorite uncle."

I can't thank him enough for chatting. I know he

is doing it for me. I even forgive him for messing up the Disney character's name and manage to smile at him. I really need something to focus on because I do feel like I want to puke. The love he has for his niece is obvious. "That's really sweet of you, Derek. I wish I had an uncle like you growing up."

"Well, my sister and I were really close growing up. She practically raised me, as my parents worked a lot. I want to be a good uncle to her daughter. Besides, I doubt I'll ever have a kid, so Maddison is about as close to a daughter as I'll get."

"Why would you say that?"

He shrugs. "I love my job too much to give enough time to a woman."

"Oh, please, you just haven't found the right one yet. When you do, things will change."

He lets out a long breath. "You may have a point. I thought Logan was going to be a lone wolf up on his mountain until you came along."

"I'm happy," I smile up at him, "and you will be too someday."

"All right, enough *chick chat*. It's show time." He holds the door open for me. "No matter what happens up there, Savannah, I'm right there with you."

"Thanks, Derek." I squeeze his arm, happy to have him with me, and extremely happy now that Blackstone is watching and listening.

We ride the elevator up to the penthouse. The doors open, and there is my father wearing his usual black suit with a glass of scotch in his hand.

Chapter Seven

"Hello, dear. Come in, come in." He gives me an awkward hug then takes my jacket. I see his hand run along the pockets.

"Father." I nod, glancing around and noting that everything looks the same.

"Captain Rent, thank you for joining us this evening." My father shakes his hand.

I try not to let it bother me that my father knows Derek's rank. I'm guessing he did his homework before we came over this evening.

After my father makes us a drink along with his small talk, the doorbell rings, making my stomach drop into my lap.

"Are you expecting someone?" Derek asks, standing at my side.

My father rises and gives us a warm smile. "Actually, yes."

I stand, glancing at Derek, who looks as worried as I am. I thought this was a private dinner.

"Savannah?" I hear her voice and I nearly drop my drink. "Is that really you?"

"Lynn?" I can barely speak as she runs over and wraps her arms around me, embracing me in that familiar hug I missed dearly. She still looks amazing. Everything matches, nothing out of place. I start to wonder about my own appearance. I quickly stop myself.

Don't go there, Savi.

"Oh my god, I thought you were dead! When your father called me to come over, I thought it was just for dinner, but when he told me you—" She pulls away and looks at me with tears in her eyes. "You look amazing!"

"Thanks, so do you." I point to Derek. "This is my friend Derek. Derek, this is my longtime friend Lynn."

"Pleased to meet you." Derek's voice is laced with discomfort. I don't blame him; I wasn't ready for this either.

"Well, well, well, look at you, spitfire." Luka holds open his arms, coming into the room and granting me a large hug. "Never thought we'd see you again."

"Luka!" I smile at him. "If you told me I would be standing here with you guys a few months ago, I wouldn't have believed it." I turn to Derek and make the introductions. Poor Derek, he does not like this.

"Okay, now, enough hovering, everyone." My father beams. "We are all excited to have her safely home. Let's get some food, and then Savannah can tell us everything that's happened."

Oh, lovely, a trip down memory lane.

Derek sits next to me, facing Lynn and Luka, and

my father sits to my left at the head of the table. After the entree is served, the questions begin.

"So you were held captive for nearly seven months, and we understand you were rescued a while ago, but why are we only seeing you now?" Lynn asks, confused. "Where were you between then and now?"

Wow, jump right in, guys.

I see Derek shift ever so slightly. I'm not sure how to answer her, but I don't need to because my father does for me.

"She was in a safe house." My mouth drops open.

"Where?" Lynn asks over the rim of her wine glass.

"I can't say," I reply, looking at my father.

"Why?"

"Rules," I answer truthfully.

"Really?" She takes a bite of her salad. "So are you and Derek dating?"

"No," Derek answers quickly.

"No, she's dating a colonel," my father says calmly. "Colonel Cole Logan, correct?"

What the hell?

I'm shocked, dumbstruck, just staring at him. "Dad, how do you know that information?" I am completely blown away by his calm comments and knowledge of my situation.

"I'm a powerful man who knows a lot of things, Savannah. I know, for instance, that your boyfriend isn't who he says he is." My father's eyes shift over to Derek's. "Just like you, Captain Rent, isn't that right?"

"I'm not following," Derek says, dropping his napkin on the table.

"Oh, well, allow me to explain then. Luka." Luka stands and hands my father a file. He flips it open and hands me a photo.

My hands shake as I look at the photo. I then look up at my father and to Luka in disbelief as I try to process what I am seeing. Cole is shaking hands with my Devil, Jose Jorge. My mouth goes dry as I look over to Derek, who is shaking his head.

"Then there's this." My father slides another picture over top of the one I'm holding. It's Derek in a coffee shop, ordering at the counter. "Note who's waiting for him in line off to his right," he says to me.

"Oh…" I whisper in shock. There is my captor, Rodrigo Heredia, the bastard, the man who ordered—and enjoyed watching—Jose beat the shit out of me to the point where I wanted to die.

"Interesting suit you have on in that picture, Derek," my father adds, taking a sip of his scotch. "Looks familiar, don't you think, Savannah?"

Holy shit, this picture is from today? My hand flies to my stomach as Derek leans into me.

"Savannah, he's setting us up."

"Pictures don't lie, Derek," my father hisses like a cat about to attack.

I shake my head, feeling faint as my blood doesn't seem to be reaching my brain. "Derek, please explain. How can this be? Tell me you didn't know he was there." I feel my eyes water as I hold up Cole's picture. "Explain this, please. This isn't making sense. How could he?"

Shattered

Derek's eyes are full of panic. "No, Savannah. You know Cole, he would never hurt you, he loves—"

Pop! Pop!

Crimson liquid sprays across my body. My ears are the ringing, and everything seems to move in slow motion. I turn my eyes to my father, who is holding a gun, then to Lynn and Luka, who are staring at the table. My gaze travels over to Derek, who is slumped in his chair, head flopped backward with a huge, gaping hole in the center of his forehead. Blood drains over his open eyes, down his nose, along his neck, and into his shirt.

The entire room is silent except for the ringing in my head. I try to focus on what is happening. My brain fights to process this moment.

"Savannah!" my father orders. "Look at me."

I unglue my eyes from Derek and somehow do as I'm told.

"Are you being tracked?"

I can feel panic start in my feet and travel through me like the bullet that is now nuzzled into Derek's skull.

"Are. You. Being. Tracked?" I can hear him, but I'm not registering his words.

Derek's blood is in my steak.

Derek's brain is everywhere.

Derek was just speaking to me, and now he's not.

Derek is dead.

My father shot Derek.

My father just shot Derek Rent.

My father pointed a gun and shot my friend.

Derek is dead.

My brain keeps looping. I'm on a merry-go-round that I can't get off.

Someone's hands feel all along my sides, sliding over my arms and down my legs. My shoes are being removed and checked and placed back on. It's Lynn. What is she doing?

"I don't feel any wires, Doug," Lynn says from her knees. "She's clean."

"I doubt that," Luka mutters, coming to my side. "They wouldn't let her come here unprotected."

"Savannah," my father snaps at me, making me look over, "Derek and Cole were in negotiations with the men who took you. They were going to hand you over for a price. The American wants you. His men are the ones who kidnapped you. He came after me...us," he points to Lynn and Luka, "saying we needed to pay for what was taken from him. They were blackmailing me for the money. I tried to pay, but it was never enough. They nearly sucked me dry. All I wanted was to get you back, but I couldn't find you. No one could." He leans toward my frozen body. "I will not let them take you away from me again. Derek wouldn't have let you stay without a fight."

This doesn't make sense. I can't get my brain to work. I need to snap out of the fog.

My hands fly to my chain but it doesn't feel right. It doesn't give me the comfort I need.

"The necklace," Lynn says reaching over and tearing it from my neck. She drops it on the floor and smashes it with her heel of her shoe.

What the hell?

Lynn bends over and picks it up. "Yup, wires." She chucks it in the corner of the room and moves in front of me, looking into my eyes. "Savi, we need to leave. They know you're here, don't they?"

I don't move a muscle, then lean to the side and vomit next to her. She jumps back, gasping in disgust.

"Shock," I hear Luka say through a full mouthful of bloody meat.

I nearly vomit again.

Lynn's shiny shoes step toward me. "No shit, Luka. You're as helpful as ever."

She hands me a napkin, and that's when I see it.

Oh my god!

The silver bracelet with the heart dangling from the center. I quickly snatch the napkin and wipe my mouth in fear I'll lunge at her. I can't believe she's the mystery woman with the heart bracelet! What does this mean? Is Lynn somehow behind this? Why would she take a picture of me the same night I was taken? Why was she even there?

"We've got to move," my father orders as he pulls me to my feet, my head spinning. He eyes my pin then roughly removes it, ripping my shirt in the process. He drops it in his water glass and yanks on my limp arm to follow.

"We've got company," Luka says as we follow him into my father's personal office. "They're in the elevator."

"Let's go." Lynn wraps her arm around my waist then stops. *Shit.* She looks over at me as she unclasps the bracelet, my last tracking device, breaking it in two. Grabbing my wrist again, she leads us through a door that I've never seen before. It reminds me of the one in the safe house leading to Cole's bedroom. I force Cole out of my head. I've got to pull myself together, but I'm still reeling from the memory of Derek's lifeless body in the dining room.

After a several flights of stairs, we are in the parking lot where my father's limo is waiting.

"Savannah!" Everyone turns to see Paul holding a pistol pointed at us. "Let her go."

"You've done enough damage, Agent Paul," my father yells back.

Paul looks directly at me. "Savannah, walk toward me."

I'm so confused, and physically nothing is working. I just stand there, not sure if I am up or down, left or right. I wish I could snap out of this fog.

"More are coming," Luka whispers with his phone to his ear.

"Savannah, walk toward me," Paul repeats.

I feel my father shift as if shielding me with his body, and I hear that godforsaken *pop* noise and see Paul plummet to the ground.

"No!" I scream and try to rush over to Paul, but my father hooks his arm around my waist and pulls me to the car. "No! Paul!" He shoves me in and jumps in after me.

"Ahhhh!" I scream, trying to get out the helpless feeling that has a tight grip on me. "Why?" No one answers me.

Lynn and Luka follow, and before I know it, we're speeding out of the parking structure and down into an alleyway where we quickly switch cars.

I'm tumbling back into darkness, once again held in its teeth. Lost, alone, and once more nothing makes sense. I've served my time in hell. Why am I back here? What did I do to deserve a second round? One thing I know for sure, I fought my way out before, and I'll sure as hell do it again!

Squealing tires snap me out of my thoughts as Luka checks to see who it is.

"She must have another tracker on her," he yells.

Lynn's hands once again run along my body. I bat her hand away. I hate that she is touching me. I hate that she makes me seethe with anger because her fucking bracelet makes a noise every time she moves her arm. It makes me want to rip it off and jam it down her throat. I need to get out of here! None of this makes sense!

"Savi," she whispers, "I'm only trying to protect you."

"Don't touch me, Lynn," I hiss under my breath.

"What's wrong with you?"

"I said don't touch me." I shift to the corner of the limo, curling up in a ball.

"Savannah," Luka shouts, "I won't ask you again. Do you have a tracker on you?"

I shake my head as Luka's anger toward me brings me to see things more clearly. "It's the U.S. Army, Luka. This is what they're trained to do. You should know; you hired them."

"Hired them?" Lynn looks confused. Her eyes snap to Luka's. "Why would we hire—"

"Lynn!" Luka snaps at her.

My chest starts to rise and fall as more shit is tossed at me. "Wait…you didn't hire them? Why did they come for me then? How did they…?" My head goes light. "Oh my god…everything…everything is a friggin' lie." I start to cry and hyperventilate at the same time. Cole lied to me! "Pull over, I'm going to be sick…*pull over*!"

"No! We can't," my father shouts, grabbing a bag and shoving it on my lap.

I snatch it up, holding it tightly. "Please, will someone tell me the truth for once in my life? I demand to know the truth."

Suddenly the car stops in an alleyway and I am being pulled out and shoved into a trunk.

"Be a good girl, Savannah," my father warns.

The last thing I see is Luka's face as he slams the trunk lid down.

"Oh my god. Oh my god." My panic escalates as the car begins to move. I can hear Dr. Roberts's voice in my head. "Breathe in through your nose and out through your mouth. Panicking won't solve the problem. Stop and look at your surroundings. See what you can do to help your situation. There's always something you can do." Holy shit…my phone!

I cover the ear part when I pushed the number two and send.

"Savannah!" His voice makes me happy but it's quickly masked with confusion and hurt. "Are you there, baby?"

"Yes," I whisper, feeling so many things.

"Oh my god! Are you all right?"

"No." I start to sob. "I'm not."

"Where are you, baby? Something is blocking our transmission."

"I'm in a trunk."

"A trunk?" he nearly shouts. "Okay, did you see anything when they were putting you in there? Your surroundings? Make and model of the vehicle?"

"No." I sniff trying to hold it together.

"It's okay, baby, hang in there. John is tracking your phone now. It won't be long until we have you."

"Cole," my voice quivers, "Paul?"

"He's all right. Bullet hit his vest, just stunned him a little."

"Derek is—"

"Yeah, we saw." There's a pause. "I can explain that picture, baby, it—"

"Don't," I interrupt. "I can't handle any more lies. I'm barely holding it together."

"Savannah, no—"

I pull my guard up. "Promise me that if Blackstone finds me alive, you'll let me go. I deserve a few years of happiness." My words are rushed in case they are my last. "I love you, Cole, and that's what hurts the most."

"He's feeding you lies, Savannah. I'm coming for you, and when I get there I'll prove I'm still your knight." My chest clenches as his words tug on my heart.

"We stopped! Cole, the car stopped!" My breathing picks up again. "Oh god, I don't want to die."

"You're not going to die, Savannah. I see where

you are. I'm roughly twenty minutes behind you."

Oh shit.

"I hear footsteps."

"Hide your phone, but don't hang up."

I quickly shove it into my bra just as the trunk opens. A man I've never seen before stares in at me.

"Savanna Miller?" he asks in a thick Hispanic accent. I'm frozen, paralyzed in fear. He grabs me and slaps me across the face. "I asked you a question. Is your name Savannah Miller?"

"Y-yes," I cry out.

He glances at a picture then pulls out a needle.

"No! No, no, no, no, please! Don't!" I scream. "pleaseeeee!" It doesn't make a lick of difference. He shoves the needle into my arm anyway.

A moment later I'm staring at a dim light peeking through a crack as I quickly drift off, knowing it's a one way ticket to hell.

Chapter Eight

Cole

Cole listens as her sobs slow and finally go quiet. Thankfully, Keith is driving, because Cole is finding it impossible to focus on anything but Savannah.

"I will take down her father and everyone with him," Cole curses as he flexes his hands on his lap.

John is clicking away on a computer in the back seat while Mark is making phone calls to Border Patrol, trying to find out if The American is in the United States or Mexico.

Seconds. Minutes. Hours. There is still no sound from Savannah. Cole nearly loses it a few times, wondering if she is alive or not. Mark has to talk him down several times. They can't call in local PD or the FBI in case someone is listening or watching. The risks are too high.

Cole finally leans back and closes his eyes, trying to remember every single part of Savannah. The one thing that comes to his mind above all else is how those deep, dark eyes of hers seem to find him even in a sea of people. God, he loves her eyes. They are hypnotic and they are his. He slips off, remembering her…

"Good morning, Colonel," Savannah's low voice makes his eyes filter open. He grins when he sees she is dressed in his army hat and button up uniform shirt, which is conveniently left undone, showing off the sides of her perfect breasts. "Time to do your morning workout."

He shakes his head as he goes to grab her. She leans back, holding up a finger.

"No, no, Colonel," her lips spread into a sexy smile, "drop and give me twenty."

His hands rush to her hips, lifting her in the air sitting her down on his growing erection. "You look damn fine in this." He fingers the shirt. "With what I have planned for you, I'm never going to wash it."

She leans down, her hair falling all around them. "Now, that, Colonel, sounds like a damn fine plan." She lifts her hips, slipping him inside her. His eyes roll back as she feeds him all the way in. She's more than ready, making everything heighten. Her body starts to move in a sexy weave and he peeks at the mirror facing them. Fuck him, it's one incredible sight. The way she arches her back makes him grow even harder. Her hands go to his hair, clutching a handful while biting her lip with a moan. One hand moves to her hip, helping her rock, the other to her breast, giving it a little squeeze. She's a fucking perfect wet dream. "Cole…"

"Logan," John whispers from the back seat, pulling him from his dream and filling him with emptiness that comes with his reality.

Cole's eyes pop open. He glances at the clock and sees he's been out for nearly three hours. "Yeah, John."

"They stopped at a hotel."

Cole sits up straighter. "Which one?"

"The Hilton, fourth floor." John reads off the address and Keith immediately heads in that direction.

When they arrive, they pull up into the driveway and do a sweep of the cars. Nothing seems out of the ordinary. The four of them head into the lobby. Cole and Keith approach the front desk.

"Hi, and welcome to The Hilton West Virginia. How can I help you this evening?"

Cole sees the young woman look him up and down as he approaches her. "Perfect," he mutters to himself. "A friend of ours checked in about thirty minutes ago. I forget his room number, but I was wondering if you could help me out?" After flirting for an endless ten minutes, he finally gets the room number.

They pile into the elevator and make their way down the hallway on the fourth floor. A man dressed in a room service uniform comes out of a room. Cole grabs his arm and whispers in his ear that they need his help and flashes his military badge.

"Yeah o-okay," the guy stutters.

"Knock," Cole orders when they stop in front of room 402.

The guy knocks and announces room service. Nothing. He knocks again, and still nothing.

"Excuse me? Can I help you?" a man dressed in a suit asks them as he approaches. "I'm the night manager. Are you gentlemen guests here?"

"No," Cole answers quickly, "but we have reason to believe a woman is being held against her will in this room."

"Are you the police?"

"No, sir. We're with U.S. Army Special Forces," Mark chimes in, knowing that normally gets people's attention. "We need to see inside that room."

"Well, I need to see some proof—"

"Agent John," Cole snaps out, "perhaps Channel Five News would like to hear about how The Hilton is allowing a man to rape a young woman with the manager's knowledge. What's your name, sir?"

"No, no, that won't be necessary." He pulls out a master key and opens the door. Cole barges through first, weapon drawn. His stomach sinks when he sees the bed.

"Oh, shit, shit, shit!" Cole hisses, turning to Mark and feeling helpless.

Mark picks up the note resting on Savannah's cell phone.

I expected more from the U.S. Army.
The girl has been bought and paid for.
She's long gone.

"They just gained an hour and twenty on us,"

John says quietly behind them. "After talking with the manager, I got a description. It was a Hispanic man who rented the room alone. He did say he was in and out in a matter of minutes. He's sending me the surveillance footage as we speak."

"All right." Keith nods at him, then looks at Cole. "Let's focus on the fact that they need Savannah alive."

They make their way back to their truck and head south on the interstate. Cole's stomach is a ball of fire in his gut. This is a far cry from when he rescued Savannah the first time, as his heart wasn't *as* invested. Yes, the moment he saw her picture in that file he was drawn to her...but now, she is his life, the air he breathes, the reason to come home from a mission. Life isn't worth living if she isn't in it.

John speaks up. "I have a location on their vehicle. Fuck, they're at a private airport."

"I'm on it," Mark says, pulling out his cell phone.

***

Savannah

I feel something warm caress my face, drawing me up and away from the darkness that is consuming me. My head hurts and my mouth is dry. I start to moan. Everything feels terrible, like I was out drinking the night before, but I know that isn't true. My eyes flutter open and I focus on a green wall in front of me.

"Huh?" I mutter. "Wh-where am I?"

"Shhhh, Savannah, you're right where you should be." Her voice rings through my ears.

Lynn.

The last god-knows-how-many hours come flooding back to me. I try to move away, but her hands keep me on the bed.

"It's okay, sweetie, take a few moments to let the drug wear off."

It takes all my effort, but I pull away and roll off the bed, hitting the floor like a wet rag. Ouch! With every passing second I can feel the drug leaving my system. I tug my heavy body off the floor and shift to lean against the opposite wall.

We sit staring at one another for a long time. I finally clear my throat, wanting some fucking answers.

"Your bracelet." I point and watch her quickly cover it with her free hand. "Is that new?"

"Sort of." She forces a smile. She's lying or avoiding the truth.

I pull my leaden legs up to my chest. "Lynn, I've known you forever. You wouldn't have bought that for yourself. So who bought it for you?" I watch as her face goes from friendly to angry.

"A friend."

I shake my head, feeling tears pool in my eyes. "I know you took my picture the night I was taken, Lynn. But I want to know why."

Her face hardens. "I did it for proof."

"Proof of what?"

She leans forward. "Proof that you were out drinking again, and proof that you were with Joe

Might."

I skip the comment about the drinking and focus in on what really confuses me. "Joe Might? The new client?"

"Yes."

"What does he have to do with anything?"

She pushes off from the bed and stands by the window. "I hired him to take you out and have you returned at home at a certain time."

I think back to that night. I remember Joe asked me to go to dinner. We had both skipped out on a very boring meeting. I drop my head to my knees, trying to accept what she is telling me.

"I-I don't understand, Lynn. Why on earth would you do that?"

Lynn sighs, acting like she's annoyed that I can't keep up. "Fuck, Savannah, you had the perfect life, damn it! You had a father who made a ton of money, you got a crap load of attention, and all you had to do was stand there and look pretty. All he ever asked of you was to help a bit with his campaign, but no, you had to whine and bitch about it to me!" She makes a face. "Oh, Lynn, I hate being in the media. Oh, Lynn, I hate all the attention. Oh, Lynn, they think I'm a drunk, blah, blah, blah." She stomps her foot like a child. "You had it so good, but were you happy? No! You couldn't see past your own nose. It was always about poor Savannah. Christ, it made me so pissed!"

As everything comes pouring out of her, all I can do is stare at my best friend. I considered her like a sister for years, and to hear the poison in her voice is shocking. To hear someone you love speak to you like this with such obvious hatred is hard to grasp. How she despises me. Yet again, lies are being told; it is incredibly heartbreaking.

"If I was such a terrible friend, Lynn, why did you stick with me for so long?"

"Fame." She shrugs like I should have connected the dots. "You were going to take me places, and I knew I could benefit, until you started fucking up in the media. That's when everything changed, that's when I knew a decision needed to be made."

The perfect storm is starting to brew inside me, tilting my world off its axis. "Decision?"

"Yes, Savannah, you were bringing everyone down with all your failures, so I stepped up to the plate. I knew someone who knew someone who was involved in human trafficking. Small world, hey?" She chuckles to herself. "So I made some calls, and lo and behold, seems the Mayor of New York's daughter was a sweet little prize to get. So I hired Joe Might, a friend of mine, to pose as a potential buyer and make sure you arrived at your condo at the right time. I knew you would go get the files. You were always on top of things. You were always so OCD when it came to your job." She rolls her eyes in disgust. "Then poof, you were gone." She laughs. "Like a magic trick, now you see her, now you don't."

That storm finally breaks, and I jump up and grab her by the hair, the two of us falling on the floor as I punch and kick and hit her, feeling the anger fueling my muscles. I'm sick of the lies, sick of being a victim. She certainly wasn't expecting it, and I get quite a few good ones in before something cracks me in the head and everything goes black.

"*Perra*." His voice jolts me from my sleep. "Oh, sweet *perra*, you came back."

I quickly sit up and take in my surroundings. I'm in an attractive room with Spanish décor. Sunlight is streaming in through a large window. It's hot. I'm sweating. I wipe my forehead and smell something funny. I realize I'm not alone in my bed. I scramble to my feet, seeing the blood. Oh my god, there's so much blood! I'm covered in it. My hair, my hands, my arms, my legs. My fingers shake as I tug the corner of the sheet that's closest to me. I need to know who it is. Dark hair peeks out. He is turned away from me. I see his shoulders, back, and waist. I drop the sheet and round the bed. I don't have to see his face to know who it is. My hands cover my mouth as vomit spews out of me.

"No!" I heave and wail at the same time. This can't be happening! The door opens quickly, and I see The American dressed in shorts and a t-shirt staring at me.

"You did this, you know." He points with his chin toward the jelly-like body. "If you had just given yourself over to me in the first place, Agent Mark Lopez would still be alive."

"Fuck you," I hiss, wiping my mouth free of vomit. "Fuck all of you."

He walks toward me as I raise my chin to meet his stare. His shoulder rises and he punches me square in the face. I feel myself falling, but I never hit the ground. I just keep falling…

I jolt straight up, trying to make sense of what's going on. I feel around the bed, empty. I see a window, but it looks different than the one I saw before, and it is night. What? So was I dreaming before? Is Mark alive?

Pushing the covers away, I see I'm still in my own clothes. They're dirty, but at least they are mine.

"Oh, good, you're awake," a voice says, coming out of what looks like a bathroom. Luka approaches, holding out a bag. "Here." He sits the Nordstrom bag in front of me. "We need to meet downstairs in twenty. That should be enough time for you to shower, change, and be ready for the exchange."

"Exchange?" I blurt out, looking around the room.

Luka nods as he sits a cup of coffee on the table next to the window. "Yes, Savannah. You've been bought and paid for. We just need to make sure all the little details are properly checked out before we hand over our, for want of a better word, ace."

My head is shaking back and forth. It seems nothing in my life can be trusted. In disbelief, I listen to someone else I considered a good friend—an uncle, even—talk about selling me like I'm nothing to him at all but a piece of merchandise. The memory of the truck flickers. "Why the trunk? If I'm still your so-called ace, why did you hand me over to that man? Why risk it?"

He taps his head. "We had to risk it. Your boyfriend's team was hot on our trail. We needed to throw them off, so we hired a friend to take you for a joy ride." He shakes his head and smiles. "It wasn't until he heard you talking on that cell phone that he decided to do the hotel trick. He dropped you off to us before he went to the hotel and left a little note for Logan to find. It worked like a charm. Meanwhile, we hopped the first plane to TJ, and you are now lost in a sea of a million people."

Tijuana? Mexico...The blood drains to my toes. I promised myself I'd never step over the Mexican border again as long as I lived. I've experienced enough hell here for a lifetime, but here I am being handed over to The American in the one place I hate beyond all else. I can't do this. Not again. I just can't. I have to do something.

"Okay," Luka slaps his hands together, making me jump, "let's go." He stares at me as I sit like a stone. "You need some help with that?" He smirks and points to my blouse. My eyes shoot to his, more shocked than ever. Luka has never said anything sexual to me before. Never even hinted at it. He really was like an uncle to me. It must show on my face, because he shrugs. "Not like I haven't thought about it before, Savannah. I'm only human. Can't blame a man for trying." I want to be sick again...or was I sick before? I can't tell if that was a dream.

I grab the bag and hurry to the restroom, slamming the door behind me. I turn on the water and peel my clothes off and toss them on the floor. I'm not sure when I'll have a chance to shower again, so I take my time. I find a razor, body wash, shampoo, and conditioner, and with my brain on overdrive I put them to good use.

I look at myself in the mirror, my hair almost dry from the heat blasting in through the tiny window. A light pink dress hits slightly above my knees, and

I'm wearing cream color heels. I wonder if Luka was the one who bought the panties and matching bra. The thought makes me want to throw something at the mirror. My eyes focus on the razor beside the soap dish. I examine it, then take the thin comb and snap the skinny blades out. They drop into my hand in one small unit. I shrug out of the top of the dress, taking the sharp blade and cutting into the first layer of lace on the bra. Just large enough to tuck the blade inside so it's undetectable. I certainly won't be able to defend myself with it, but I am desperate enough to take anything useful, and I have other ideas if there is any possibility I'm going to be held in another cell. I set the handle of the razor back down so it looks normal and peek out the miniscule window.

All I can see are rows and rows of tin roofs. But I do spot a plane landing off in the distance. I must be close to the airport. Two streets down, I see a convenience store with a payphone outside. I need to get out of here! I nearly sob when I hear Luka's voice through the door telling me it's time to go. I push on the glass, not that I could ever fit through it, and scream, hoping someone can hear me. A pair of hands grab my wrists, pulling them down roughly.

"Not this time, Savannah. This time you play by our rules." He yanks me to follow, and somehow I do. He shoves me into the elevator and slams his hand over the L button. "Christ, woman, I wish you would just do as you're told!"

I stare at the side of his face, wanting so badly to kick him in the stomach. "Oh, I'm sorry, Luka. Should I just nod and smile as you hand me over to

Shattered

The American like I'm some piece of meat?"

"Shut up, Savannah," he grits out.

"Fuck you, Luka!" I snap back without thinking.

Suddenly he's wrapping his hands around my throat, slamming me back into the elevator wall. Hard. My head snaps forward from the impact. I cry out, but his lips smash into mine as his grip around my neck tightens. My hands claw at his shirt, but he doesn't stop. He thrusts his tongue forward as I try to wiggle free. He's too strong. Oh god, this is disgusting. Finally my brain kicks into action and I jam my knee with all the force I have into his tiny testicles. Immediately he lets go, falling backward. I gasp heavily, trying to get a full breath of air into my screaming lungs, and drop to my knees.

"Fucking bitch!" He groans above me as he drives his fist into my cheek. My teeth clench at the impact, and pain shoots everywhere. This is way too much like my last 'trip to Mexico.' My brain snaps to full alert. I need to be able to fight, I need to stay focused. The door opens and I see a blurry figure standing in front of me.

"What the fuck!" my father yells out. I feel his hands on me, lifting me to my feet. I have a small moment where I think my father might actually take pity on me, take me home and protect me from these monsters. "Are you insane? She needs to be in mint condition. If he thinks we've hurt her in any way, he may back out of the deal." So much for 'daddy dearest.' *I'm a fool.*

"What the shit is taking so long?" Lynn shouts from behind us. "We have four minutes before he shows up. Let's move." I feel her cast-iron grip on my arm, tugging me toward the restaurant. I notice the staff won't make eye contact with me, and I think I may be the only guest.

Lynn drops me into a wooden seat as the other three sit around the table. I stare at the yellow flower floating on top of the water in a square clear jar.

"Savannah?" Lynn hisses at me. I look over as she opens her purse and shows me her handgun. Weapons don't really scare me anymore, so I don't react. "You try and run, I'll shoot you. I have excellent aim."

"Good for you, Lynn," I whisper with a sigh. I'm tired of her now. I look back at the flower, thinking about how much it reminds me of myself at the moment, just floating in a world I have no control over, and helpless to whatever fate comes my way. We're both screwed.

Mark, John, Paul, Keith, Abigail, June, Sue, Daniel, Scoot, Mike, Frank, Derek…Cole. I keep reciting their names over and over, trying to keep my brain sharp. I will not get lost again, I will not get lost in my mind. I need to stay in the present. Mark, John, Paul, Keith…My head turns to my father.

"How, Dad?" I shake my head. "Please just tell me how you can do this to your own daughter. Do I really mean nothing to you?" I hate that my voice cracks at the end.

He sips his coffee, glancing at Luka, then to me. "It's just business, Savannah. Please don't get all emotional right now. I need you to be on your best behavior."

Shattered

It's not a good feeling when your heart breaks in two, but the anger fuses it back together in a matter of seconds. I bite the inside of my cheek to hold back the words, but it doesn't work. My eyes narrow in on his, and I let fly. "I hope you rot in hell, you pathetic excuse for a father! Mom was right, you were never much of a man." This isn't true, but I know it will hurt his pride.

He quickly stands and makes his way over to me and slaps me across the face. I fall out of the chair, hitting the floor and laughing hysterically. This time Lynn comes over, and I think she's going to help me to my feet, but she kicks my side hard. I cry out, coughing and trying to catch my breath. Well, if my plan was to get them all to hit me, it worked. I hope if I look like shit there'll be some hell to pay from The American.

I roll to my side, tucking my legs up to my stomach. "Mark, John, Paul, Keith." I start my chant but freeze when two cobra heads stop inches from my face. Fear dances around my stomach, replacing the pain of my possibly fractured ribs. He bends down and wipes the hair out of my face. Tears are streaming from my eyes now, big hot tears. My family is selling me, The American bought me, the love of my life may have betrayed me, and Derek is dead because of me! All I want is to do is disappear, have something swallow me up, because *anything* is better than the outcome of this.

"Who did this?" The American asks in a booming voice, looking at me, but I just shake. He reaches out and lifts me carefully and places me on the chair. This action scares me, as it feels almost tender, and for some reason that makes me even more frightened of him. I tense and sit awkwardly in the chair with my eyes glued to the floor.

"Ms. Miller." I look up and see a white man, who looks like a lighter version of Mike, black and white tattoos from head to toe, and big and beefy. I'm taking it he's the muscle for The American. He gives me a tight smile then glares at the rest of the group. He continues to stand by my side as Luka decides to start the conversation off.

"So, here she is. We held up our end of the bargain, and now it's time for you to do the same." Luka yanks at his tie, clearly uncomfortable in The American's stare.

Lynn tosses out her best smile. "So why don't you just make the call to Rodrigo, and we can all be home in time for tea?"

I shake my head, thinking I've never seen Lynn drink a cup of friggin' tea in her life. The table is painfully quiet. All I can hear is the pounding in my head, and I feel my cheek pulsing to my rapid heartbeat. I move without thinking, making everyone look at me. I hesitate but slowly reach into my glass of water and start piling up ice cubes into my cloth napkin, then hold my makeshift icepack to my cheek and eye, tensing in pain. Christ, it hurts.

Finally, The American, who is now watching me closely, turns to look at the rest of them. "Who hit her eye?" His words are spoken with such tightly controlled anger it makes me suck in my breath. "Three, two…"

"Luka!" Lynn blurts out, pointing to him across the table. You can actually see the blood drain from

Shattered

Luka's face and it twists with her betrayal.

The American pulls out a pistol, points it at Luka's skull, and pulls the trigger. His body flies backward to the floor. Lynn is screaming, my father is frozen, and I'm numb, beyond caring. The American and his muscle just sit there acting like nothing has happened, exactly how my father, Lynn, and Luka were when Derek was shot. *Karma.*

The American tucks his gun away. "When we are clear, I will call Rodrigo and tell them the deal is done." He stands and buttons up his suit jacket. "But I warn you, if you so much as step in my way, I will not hesitate to kill you like I did your friend." He takes my hand, pulling me up to my feet. "Is there anything you would like to say, Savannah?"

I stare up at him. "To which group of animals are you referring?"

He smiles gently like he's in love with me. "Less sass, my love. I can be good to you, and you do not want to anger me." His smile may be gentle, but his eyes have a glint of steel. "I can be very, very bad when I am angry, my sweet, but it is your call."

I nearly laugh at that. "I'm not your love, nor am I sweet, and you can do anything you want to me because, frankly, I don't care. It's all been done before."

My father stands and holds up his hands. "Savi, just do as you're told, please."

I shake my head in utter disbelief. "Really, *Douglas*, you want to play the concerned father now? Save it." I turn to Lynn. "So help me God, I hope this all comes crashing down on top of you both. I hope you burn in hell, you evil pieces of shit." I turn on my heel and exit the room with the muscle coming up behind me quickly.

"Ms. Miller," he calls out. I stop, knowing there's no point. I've been bought and paid for. The American comes up to me, gripping a firm hand around the back of my neck.

"You will never turn your back to me again," he whispers for only the three of us to hear. "Now, I have some work to do. Tim here will make sure you get home safely, where you will wait for me in our room, with nothing on. Oh, and, love, I like you to be smooth down south." His eyes drop to my crotch. He leans in, grips my head, and kisses me hard. I try to fight it, but he digs his thumb into my shoulder, making me cry and go limp. Once he's finished, he pushes me into Tim's grip. "I'll be home tonight. Make sure she's ready for me."

"Yes, sir." Tim nods and wraps his huge hand around my wrist.

I spit on the ground once he's gone. Tim says nothing as he pushes me into the elevator and we go down to the parking level. He opens the door of a black town car and helps me in. I notice once the door is closed, it locks. Tim slips into the driver's seat, starts the car, and pulls into traffic.

That's when I shatter into a million pieces. A horrible sob bursts from my throat and I start to shut down. Mark, John, Paul, Keith, Abigail, June, Sue, Daniel, Scoot, Mike, Frank, Derek, Cole...but it doesn't work. I can feel myself slipping away.

I barely feel the car stop. I only blink a few times when Tim climbs into the back seat with me. He holds up his hands, showing me he won't hurt me.

Shattered

"Here." He opens a little black bag and shows me the label Extra Strength Tylenol. I look at him, confused. There has to be a catch. "Take three, miss, you'll need it. Are your ribs all right?" I shake my head no, because honestly they aren't. He nods then hands me a bottle of water, removing the lid.

"Why do you work for him?" I'm not really sure why I ask, but I want to know and I feel like I need to say something.

He tucks the Tylenol away, avoiding eye contact. "It wasn't a choice."

Chapter Nine

Cole

Cole raises his gloved hand up into the air, waiting for Mario to get into position. Paul and John are sprawled out on the couches, beyond beat from sparring with him earlier.

"Logan, you've been at this for over three hours." Mario shakes his head. "Your body needs a break, and god knows we do too."

"Again," Cole grunts out, still reeling with the decision to come home. It was the hardest decision, but they need to regroup and find what resources they can use.

Mario sighs and they continue to box for the next fifty minutes until he finally calls it quits. Cole, still with energy to burn, hits the free weights until he's physically exhausted.

After a cold shower, he finally heads to his office and pours himself a double. He tries hard to pretend Savannah is in his bedroom waiting for him to join her, her eyes wild with excitement as she peels off his clothes like it's the first time. The thought nearly brings him to his knees. God, he loves her…and now…He shakes his head trying to clear it. Then he lets out a long stream of air and makes a call.

"I wondered when I was going to hear from you." Frank's voice is quieter than normal.

Cole sips his brandy. "Anything?"

"Luka Donavan didn't return with the Mayor or Lynn." He sighs. "We had a tail on them, but he only caught up with them at the airport. The Mayor told the press that he and Lynn were on a much-needed vacation from the media. They were at the TJ airport."

"So you have nothing?"

There's a pause.

"She's been handed over, Logan. She was bought and paid for and, we believe, delivered to The American." Frank clears his throat. "Whatever you need."

"Blackstone will be shipping out at twenty hundred. I want your team, Frank. I want Eagle Eye."

"Consider it done."

"I need to make a trip to Texas too."

"Cindy?"

"Yeah, she knows a lot. I'll do what I have to."

"I agree."

Cole slams back the rest of his drink and sends out a text telling Blackstone they're leaving in sixty minutes. He closes his eyes and shifts into survival mode.

The house is quiet; everyone seems to be busy. He finds his mother in the kitchen stirring her tea and staring out the window. She turns when she hears his footsteps, and tears leak out of the corners of her eyes. Batting them away, she tries to be strong.

"She's a fighter, Cole."

"That she is." He slumps onto the stool, feeling the weight of the world falling all around him.

His mother slides a comforting hand over his shoulder. "She thought she was doing the right thing. You can't blame her for loving you too much."

"I don't."

"It's easy to walk into the lion's den when you don't know the lion is there."

"Trust me, Mother, she's well aware he's home now."

"Logan." Mark's voice makes his head snap up. Mark's puffy eyes give more away than he'd probably like to let on. "Umm, can I get you to look over the map with me?" Cole nods and stands as he forces a smile at his mom and goes to walk by Mark. Mark grabs his arm and wraps him in a hug, throwing Cole off. "I'm sorry," Mark whispers in a sob, holding him tightly, "I'm so sorry, Cole." Cole clings to his best friend, his brother, and finally lets out a little cry of his own.

***

Savannah

I keep my eyes closed, trying to hold the panic at bay. I start with Cole's shaggy, silky hair just long

Shattered

enough that I can get the perfect grip to haul him to my mouth. His dark eyes, his perfect nose, his lips, his smile that…I jolt forward as the car comes to a stop. I peer out the window and see we're in the middle of nowhere, sitting in front of two huge cast-iron gates. I memorize the make of the security system and carefully watch Tim punch 55725 into the key pad. The gates swing open and we start to roll forward down a long, dusty driveway.

The house strikes me as odd, though, as it looks like a home straight out of Louisiana. It has two stories and is painted white with green shutters. There are six pillars in the front, and two wrap-around balconies, one on top and one on the bottom. Lord, this place is massive.

Then it dawns on me this is my new prison. Sure, it's a step up from the last one, but nonetheless, it's still a prison.

There are men with rifles scattered across the yard, and security cameras pointing in every direction. German shepherds on leads are sniffing the ground. One catches my scent and starts to growl as Tim holds the door open, watching me crumble, falling apart all over again. He moves to help me out carefully. He's oddly gentle for such a big man.

He opens the door for me and nods at the butler and wait staff. They quickly scurry out of sight. Tim leads me upstairs to a bedroom immediately to the left. He tells me it's my room and that anything I need will be in the bathroom. I think back to what The American said. *Make sure she's ready for me.* I freeze, stuck mid-step.

"I can't do this, Tim." I start to shake. "Please, please get me out of here!" I turn to him with pleading eyes. "I don't belong here. I don't want to be here. I don't want that man touching me…" Tim reaches for my elbow, pulling me across the room and into the bathroom. He closes the door and holds a finger up to his mouth, urging me to be quiet.

He leans in close, making me stiffen. "Cry," he whispers, pulling back to look into my eyes with a strange expression. "When he goes to touch you, cry and say no. He won't be able to do it. Denton is one evil fucker, but the one thing he won't do is touch a woman against her will."

I blink a few times and try to absorb what he just said. Denton? So The American's name is Denton. "Why?" I struggle to get my thoughts in order. "Why in the hell would he bring me here? Does he really think I would let him sleep with me?"

Tim shakes his head slowly then checks his watch. "Denton's smart." He taps his head. "Very, very smart. That's why all these years no one's been able to touch him. He'll use mind games to control you, and before you know it he'll get you into his bed. Denton can convince a priest to kill; he's that good at manipulation."

"Why does it sound like I'm not the first woman he's had here?"

"You're the fifth."

"Fifth!" I hiss, only to have Tim's huge hand wrap around my mouth.

He closes his eyes like he's regretting telling me anything. "Yes, so you won't be alone here in this house." *Wait! The girls are here?* "You can't trust

Shattered

them, Savannah, they're all brainwashed, and whatever you say to them they will tell Denton, and you'll be punished." He drops his hand. "Punished in worse ways than when you were with Rodrigo."

My eyes flicker with fear as I scan the bathroom. "Tim, please tell me how to get out of here. I won't last. I'll end it now."

Stepping away from me and turning on the shower, letting hot steam fill the room, he motions for me to move away from the door and into a walk-in closet at the back of the bathroom. He closes the doors behind us and turns on the tiny light. I don't know why, but I don't feel nervous with Tim, maybe because he reminds of the guys back at the house. Big, but kind.

"Look, Savannah, I'm not a bad person. I never asked to work for the Cartel. I was just born into this life. My father was a runner for cocaine when he met my mother and got her pregnant. Trouble was, when she found out who my father really was, she tried to leave him. They only let her live until I was born." His eyes shift downward for a moment. "I found out later my father was the one who killed my mother. I'll spare you the details." *Thanks*. "After that, my father gained the trust of the higher-ups and soon ran a few groups smuggling weapons and people in and out. If I wanted to live, I had to keep my head down and my mouth shut. They started me out small, but once they realized I could slip through the border with no problem, I was transferred to work with my father, and from there to here. Denton has known me for a few years, and a year ago told me I was going to be working for him. You don't say no to Denton. I hate it here, I hate those women. Two of them I'm convinced played Denton, because they were evil from day one, and the other three are way past trying to live."

"I'm really sorry for your mother, Tim."

"Thank you, as I am for your mother."

This throws me. "You know my mother is dead?"

"I know all about you, Savannah, down to your shoe size."

"Well, that's not incredibly creepy," I mutter sarcastically.

"It's my job, just like it is for Logan's company."

My breath gets caught in my throat. Cole's name being uttered from Tim's lips is unnerving. "You know about Logan?"

"I know he's Special Forces. I know what he specializes in. I know that as soon as he slips back into the States, he drops off the radar just like Denton does. Denton has been trying to track Logan's group for years, but he hasn't succeeded. When Denton found out Logan had you, well, let's just say my job's been pretty miserable."

I sink onto a small chair, as my legs can no longer hold my weight. I'm just going to say it. "Tim, you must know, Logan is a good man."

"I do," he interrupts, making me pause and stare for a moment.

"Okay." I nod. "Well, you say you can slip across the border without being seen. Can you help me get out of here and back home?" I'm careful not to say where home is.

"You want to go home?" His eyebrow rises. "Back to your father? Back to that bitch Lynn?"

"No." I stand. "I want to go back to the States where I can live a real life that's mine." He smiles slightly. I'm guessing that's the answer he was looking for.

"You'll never get that while Denton is alive."

I feel bold. "Then let's deal with that problem." His eyes pop open. "Look, Tim, I've been through some real shit before. I've never killed anyone, but I know good trumps evil. You said it yourself, Denton is pure evil. Let's try and make this world just a little bit better by taking him out of it."

He stands there towering over me, studying me, thinking for a few long moments. I feel myself start to second guess if I can trust this guy. Oh shit, maybe this is a test!

"It can't happen right away," he finally says, putting his hands on his hips. "It'll be too obvious."

"How long are you thinking?"

"A few months."

"Two weeks max is all I can do."

He makes a face. "A month."

"Two weeks."

"Three."

I let out a long, shaky breath, mulling over my options. I could try and escape, but if he punishes like Tim says he does, I know I'll break. "Okay, under one condition." *Oh god, what am I agreeing to?*

"What's that?"

***

Cole

Cole clicks his radio, signaling to Blackstone that they are close to the drop-off spot. They're five minutes out when a call comes through on the satellite phone. He glances at his father, who shakes his head. No one should be calling unless something's happened. Everyone is silent; only the rev of the Land Rover engine can be heard.

"Mike?" Cole answers quietly.

"You're not going to believe this, Logan, but…go ahead."

"Cole?" Her voice smacks his stomach into a somersault and lodges it right into his throat.

"Savannah? Where are you?" He has a ton of questions but he stops himself.

"Hi." He can tell she's fighting tears.

"Hi, baby," he gets out. "Where are you?"

"I'm somewhere in TJ. Some farm with a Louisiana-looking home. Cole, his name is Denton."

"The American's?" he asks, still shocked to hear her voice.

"Yes. Luka's dead. The American killed him. I don't know where Douglas and Lynn are. I'm here at The American's house, and there are other girls here. Five others." She races on, "The American brainwashes them. He says he wants to sleep with me tonight, but…" Cole clenches his jaw so hard he's sure he cracked a tooth. "Tim is his muscle, and he's going to help me."

"Hold on." Cole is trying to take in her words, but she's talking a mile a minute. "Who's Tim?"

142

"The American's bodyguard. He said he doesn't want to help Denton anymore. Cole, he's going to help me get rid of him. It will take three weeks, then Tim will help me get back home."

Cole glances at his father and shakes his head. "Savi, I need you to listen to me. Are you near a window?"

"There's nothing for miles, Cole. Umm, Depex...the-the security key code to get through the driveway gates is, ahh, 55725."

Cole scribbles her information on his arm. "Okay, calm down, slow down. How long did you drive for?"

"I don't know. Tim gave me Tylenol for the pain, so I slept most of the way."

Cole lets out a long breath. "Baby, that wasn't Tylenol. He drugged you so you didn't know where he was taking you."

"No, Cole, Tim is going to help me."

"Why did you have to take Tylenol?" Cole asks, ignoring her last comment. *Silence.* "Savannah?"

"My family all turned on me; that's why The American killed Luka. I think my ribs are fractured. Physically I'm okay, but until Tim offered to help me I think I was mentally slipping."

Cole closes his eyes, wanting to take her pain away. "We're about to cross the border. I'm coming for you, baby. I will make sure of it." He hears her starting to cry and jams his fist into the dashboard, cracking it. John pulls the Land Rover over, getting out with the others and giving him a moment alone with her.

"I have this tiny," she hiccups, trying to find her

voice, "razor blade tucked into my bra. I thought about using it."

Cole's heart misses a beat. Leaning forward and catching himself, he pleads with her. "Please, Savannah, hold on for me, I need you. If you can take anything away from this phone call, take this. I'm coming for you. I'm in love with you, you know that! We're going to be okay. I just need you to hang on. You need to make me another Fritter."

"Yes, Colonel." Her voice suddenly changes; someone must have come into the room.

"Is there someone there?"

"Yes."

"Tim?"

"Yes."

"Just stay put, I'm coming for you. I need you to repeat after me. *"Nos encontramos mañana enfrente de la marketa con la puerta roja a las tres de la tarde."* She does, making it sound like she speaks Spanish fluently. "Perfect job. Okay, don't say a word about any of us."

"All right," she sniffs, making him want to cry himself. "Colonel?"

"Yes, baby?"

"The snowflake...that's what I'm holding onto." The line goes dead.

"You got a hit, Mike?" he asks, knowing Mike is still listening and taking down all the information Savannah rambled off.

"Burner phone. I've already started the search on the security system. I'll be in touch."

Cole drops the phone on his lap, needing a moment to comprehend everything that just happened. His heart aches thinking about her last words. The night he bought the snowflake necklace for her was the night they both declared their love for one another. It's good to know that even after all she has been through, especially after seeing that photo, she still loves him.

His father is the first to get into the Land Rover. "Tell me, is our girl all right?"

Cole wipes his eyes. He hadn't even realized they were watering while he talked to her. "We'll see." Daniel reaches over and gives his son's shoulder a tight squeeze. The rest of the guys pile in, and as John starts the engine, Cole says, "Change in plans, boys."

***

Savannah

I watch Tim slip the burner phone into his pocket. He nods toward the bathroom.

"He'll be expecting you to be clean." He makes a sorry face. "We can't have him wondering why I didn't do my job."

I look down, feeling a wave of nausea run through me. Can I really trust this man? I wonder what Cole made me repeat. I know better than to ask questions when we are not alone. Tim picks out a short dress and leaves, saying I need to be downstairs in one hour for The American's arrival.

I quickly shower, taking every so often to control my meltdowns, dress in the ridiculously short red dress, slip on what can only be described as stripper stilettos, and head downstairs. Every step makes my stomach knot tighter, makes me want to run out the front door and across the border to freedom at any cost.

A little old man, a staff member, gives me a small nod and points to where I'm supposed to go. I wonder if he knows I'm being held here against my will. I'm sure he does.

I step into a massive dining area and find myself stared down by five very scary girls who look like they're out for blood. I have no doubt that I just stepped into a new rendition of The Hunger Games. I take the open seat next to a blonde girl who snickers when I settle in.

The redhead with the bad dye job across from me makes a show of looking me over. Her drawn-on eyebrows are raised as she shoots daggers at me. Not knowing what to do with myself, I reach for my napkin and place it on my lap.

"Esta gringa thinks she has manners," Eyebrows snickers, making the rest of the girls laugh except the blonde girl next to me.

"Her name is Savannah," The American—Denton—says, his voice sucking every ounce of strength I have left out of me. "You can learn something from her, Tracy." He leans in and runs the back of his fingers down my cheek. I freeze, paralyzed in fear.

Tracy, a.k.a. Eyebrows, points her fork at me. "Shit, Denton, she doesn't even want you." She looks over at him, flashing a toothy smile. "You want me to show you how much I want you?" She opens her mouth and flicks her tongue. *Yuck.*

Shattered

"Enough, Tracy, or I'll send you upstairs again." Tracy's face drops at The American's words.

Dinner is served, and they all start to eat. I stare at the plate, feeling like I want to vomit.

"Every girl has to eat, Savannah." The American rests his hand on mine. I quickly pull it out from under his, not wanting any kind of contact with him. "Are you going to fight me every step of the way, my love?"

"I'm not your love."

"In time you will be," he says, sounding very matter of fact.

"You can't love a monster," I hiss under my breath, hearing the girls gasp.

The American closes his eyes and takes a deep breath. "You will treat me with respect, Savannah."

"Like you have with me?" I counter, fearing my not-so-silver tongue is going to get the best of me here soon.

"Leave us," he commands the rest of the girls. They quickly grab their plates and scurry out of the room. Eyebrows mutters something about the attic as she leaves, making the hair on my neck stand at attention.

I notice Tim giving me a tiny shake of the head. I don't care; I won't be here for much longer. One way or another I will be leaving this house.

A serving guy snatches my plate from in front of me as someone else removes my fork and knife.

Denton chucks his napkin on his empty plate with a deep sigh. "I don't tolerate name calling. I demand respect from you." *My god, this man has some nerve.* "So what do you have to say to me?"

Don't do it, don't do it, don't do it!

"You're insane if you think you'll get me to break like the rest of your puppets." I get to my feet, making the chair scrape along the floor. My voice is oddly steady. "You're forgetting, *Denton*, I was held captive for seven months. They didn't break me, they only made me stronger." That's a lie, but he doesn't need to know that. I tap my head and lean toward him. "Mentally and physically. So what I have to say to you, *Denton the monster*, is fuck you." I say the last two words slowly and accurately.

He runs his tongue slowly along his teeth, and I can see him vibrating. Oh, I hit a nerve. But then a smile appears, and I know I won't like what's coming next.

"I think it might be time to show you that your life isn't what you think it is." He nods to Tim, who quickly exits, returning with a laptop and a file.

Okay...

Denton opens the laptop, clicks a few buttons, and then turns it to face me.

I lean forward then freeze, seeing it's the TMZ article the woman in the elevator mentioned. My eyes trickle down to the two people kissing and I almost lose it.

Chapter Ten

My father's arm is wrapped around Lynn's waist, and his tongue is stuck down her throat. He clicks a few images, showing me different angles. No matter how many times I look away and look back, I feel betrayed. He was like a father to her! She was his other daughter! How many times have I heard him say that? I wonder if Luka knew.

"Luka was involved too," he says as if I had asked out loud. "It is said they took turns sometimes, or perhaps at the same time. Lynn was their entertainment, but it is she who is the true mastermind of this whole situation." The American swings the computer to face him and starts typing away. "You see, Savannah, your own family wanted nothing to do with you. This threesome has been going on for years. Lynn was barely of legal age when your father approached her. Lynn has ambition; she is determined to make something of herself, so she went along."

This is insane... I sink back into my chair.

"How-how could you know all of this?"

"I'll get to that right after…this." He turns the laptop around again, and I feel my feistiness fade away, leaving raw, gritty pain. "Yes, Savannah, the Colonel has been a busy man since you've been gone."

"It's…" I take a moment gathering myself, "just a picture." *Another one to add to the pile.* Deep down I know there has to be an explanation, but he hits the arrow button, showing me another one, and the knife twists a little deeper.

"I know you and the Colonel have a relationship. I saw his face when Luka mentioned your name. We tortured him for hours and got nothing, but," he raises a finger, "when Luka mentioned you sexually, he reacted. It was a telltale sign that we found his weak spot." He shrugs. "But now you're gone, and men have needs." He hits another button, showing me more. The pictures are all with the same girl. They look to be in Texas. She a beautiful blonde, with long legs, huge boobs, and she is sporting the skimpiest outfits. In every picture he's touching her in some way. The one that hurts the most is where he's tucking her hair behind her ear, gazing at her the same way he looks at me.

"How did you get these? These could be from years ago, before I met him."

The American points to a digital sign that's off in the background. Shit, two days ago.

"How?"

The American closes the computer and leans back in his chair. "Remember, Savannah, everyone has a price. Anyone can be bought." His eyes flicker with amusement at his little comment. "It's all about finding what they want. I'm a wealthy man, Savannah. I can make things happen." I shake my head. My brain is spinning, desperately looking for answers. "I got to one of the Colonel's men. He was willing to do anything for me once I knew he had three kids in University. When I handed him a wad of cash, he practically wept."

"Who?" The word was like acid on my tongue. Everyone's face from the house flickered in front of me. "York?"

"Oh, please, don't be insulting, Savannah. York was an asshole pervert who couldn't even finish the job I ordered him to do."

"He almost killed me!" I slam my hand down on the table.

The American waves a hand at me. "But he didn't, just like he didn't get the results of your blood tests online like he was supposed to. He could have done it. He was fine with hurting you, and he was fine with handing you over to me, but he was never going to give up the location of their base. So I moved on, found someone younger, someone I can trust to do some digging. I sent the word out that York was done, and he offed himself before I could get to him. One less worry to deal with."

"So who is it?"

"Who do you think?" His eyes challenge me to answer, but I'm smart enough to keep my mouth shut.

"You're bluffing."

"Am I?" He opens a file and tosses a stack of pictures at me. They slide around the table, some falling to the floor. They're all of Cole and the blonde woman. However, some are at different times of the day and she's in different outfits. Clearly she and Cole had been spending time together and recently. "Nice to know when you are in trouble you can count on him, hey?" He pats my arm. "Well, the Colonel is clearly getting his own needs taken care of." He pauses for a moment. "Your life has been a lie. Nothing is what it seems, but *this,* my love," he leans forward and gives me a hungry gaze, "this can be something real."

My head drops. I feel so tired I just want it all to end. Everything hurts. I wish I could slip away somewhere, anywhere, even if it means I have to create a false happiness. At least I can blissfully pretend life is good.

"Now, let me take you to bed. I can make you feel so much better."

That does it. I come abruptly out of my stupor and glare at him. "You touch me and I'll cut your dick off when you're sleeping. I will never sleep with you, so you wasted your money buying me. You can take your sick little twisted fantasy and shove it up your ass!"

"Oh, such a mouth. This is not like you, Savannah. You need to calm down. You have no one but me now to love you. The proof is in your past. The proof is in those pictures. Are you sure you want to threaten the person who saved you from all that? The one person who's asking you to give him a chance? I want you to be mine."

I stand. I'm done. This man is mad.

"I can never love a monster. How can you expect me to love you? You may think you can buy my body, but you can't buy my soul."

I see a flash of anger in his eyes, then he grabs my arm and drags me up the stairs to a small room in the attic, tossing me to the floor. Tim follows us and picks me up, muttering something about never speaking to The American like that. He apologizes for having to handcuff me to the wall, saying he hopes I'll only be left here for a few hours then leaves me alone with my thoughts. I can hear his footsteps as he heavily descends the steps. I lose all self-control, tucking myself into a ball, and pour my pain out through my tears.

I. Am. Done.

***

Cole

Cole shimmies himself to the edge of the roof, raising the binoculars and trying to get a visual on his target. The Red Door market is busy, so it's perfect for his men to blend in with the rest of the locals. Frank's Eagle Eye team of four is on the ground, while Blackstone is established on the rooftops. John and Paul have the entrance. Keith and Daniel have the exit, and Cole and Mark have the center.

He slides a fresh piece of cinnamon gum in his mouth as he scans the crowds. It isn't easy looking for someone they've never met before. Mike worked his magic with his contacts, and they finally came up with a name, Tim Powers. His father is heavily involved with the Cartel. *Of course.* There was even some talk that *Tim* killed his own wife after his son was born. Nice…not exactly the boy next door type. Cole glances down at the picture, studying Tim's tattoos. Most of them represent prison gangs. He has an angel on his neck and three sixes along his collarbone.

"Blackbird One to Raven One," his father's voice cracks over the radio.

"Go ahead, Blackbird." Cole raises his binoculars and scans the crowd.

"I have a visual on our subject entering from the west gate and heading toward you. Cream shirt, black hat, black pants."

"Copy that, Blackbird."

"Eagle Eye Two to Raven One. I also confirm visual on our subject. He's heading my way," one of Frank's team members adds to the radio waves.

Cole clicks his radio. "Copy that, stay in position. We follow him from here." After everyone confirms their visual on the target, they hold tight and watch his every movement, studying his mannerisms and surveying the crowd to see if he's alone.

They soon discover Tim travels in a group of four. They each carry two weapons in plain sight in the waist of their pants. Definitely not professionals, all smoking like chimneys, and one even polished off several beers and is now showing signs of being tired. Two of the four men look to be brothers and are more interested in playing on their phones than anything else. After three long hours of watching them, something finally seems to be happening. Tim Powers' back is to Cole, and he seems to be angry.

"Raven Two, are you getting this?" Cole asks Mark.

"Affirmative, the drunk is angry, saying the girl set them up and it's a waste having her handcuffed to a wall when she should be spread out..." Mark's voice trails off for a moment, making Cole blink back the idea of popping a bullet into the fucker's skull. Where the hell was she handcuffed? "Subject is yelling back, saying go get the car."

"Be ready to move. Fox One and Two, let's go." He orders Paul and John down to the SUV so they can be ready when the time comes.

Rushing to get to the car before the men get there, Daniel signals at Cole to cover him as he drops to the ground and slips a tiny tracking device to the 1993 Honda Civic that Tim arrived in. Moments later they're following the low-riding car down a busy street. Mark is in the back seat, tracking the car to make sure they have a good signal in case they lose them.

They settle into what becomes a long drive. An older couple who seems to be on a Sunday drive, as well as two other cars, are between them and the Honda, so it's an easy job to tail them without being obvious. Finally, after about two hours, the Honda pulls into a small driveway of a rundown home.

"*Mijo!*" An elderly lady comes hurrying out, kissing one of the brothers on the cheek and slapping the other upside his head.

John parks far enough away so they won't be detected, and they quickly set up their equipment in order to hear exactly what's being said.

"Tim, what's Denton's new girlfriend like?" a younger woman asks from inside the kitchen. Cole hands his father a pair of earphones as he shifts his into a better position.

"Why you want to know, Gigi?" Tim laughs. "He's not interested in you."

"Screw off," she hisses. "I just want know if she's a *gringa* like you."

The young girl shouts as someone smacks her.

"*Sí*, she's a *gringa*. Pretty little thing. Denton fought hard to get this one, but she's already in the attic. She has a mouth on her." He laughs again. "She called him a monster and said to go fuck himself." They all laugh.

The old lady makes a tisking sound as she clanks some dishes. Cole and his men flinch at how loud it is over the earphones.

"Ha! You can laugh, but I know I can give Denton what he wants. Why would he want a *gringa*? I can see myself in that grand house, just like the one from Skeleton Key. I would be wearing pretty clothes and..."

The men cut her off, laughing and teasing the woman, saying she should go there and kill the girl so Denton could see that she is the one he should be with.

Cole looks at Mark, who is the movie buff, waiting to see if he knows what the girl meant by the house from Skeleton Key. Mark clicks away on the laptop then turns it around to show him.

A Louisiana style home? Here in TJ? That's different and should be easy to find. Mark nods and gets to work, and Cole mentally kicks himself as he

Shattered

remembers Savannah mentioning it looked like that.

In the house a chair scrapes the floor as the girl asks, "So did the GI Joe crew show up?"

Someone snickers something Cole can't make out, then a cough. "No one showed. I think the girl was fucking with me, seeing if she could trust me. Too bad for her." He snorted. "She'll get hers. Denton will take his time breaking her and will enjoy himself the whole time. Denton is a sick fucker."

Mark makes a face at Cole, knowing he isn't the only one itching to get a moment alone with this guy.

As night rolls around, Cole and Mark take the first shift, and the rest pass out in a matter of minutes. One thing about being in the Army, you can fall asleep anywhere, and when you're told to sleep, you don't think twice. You find a spot and you're out. Mark trades places with John later in case Tim decides to leave in the middle of the night.

They're silent for a few hours, Cole's mind spinning with thoughts of Savi. Wondering if she's hurt, if she's wondering where he is, wondering what she ever did to deserve this life.

"I didn't think we'd be back here with Savi again," Mark whispers as he takes a bite of his power bar. "She'll forgive you, Cole." He turns to look at him. "Once you explain that photo with Rodrigo, she'll understand and forgive you." Cole shakes his head, knowing how bad that picture looks, but it had to be done. "She loves you," Mark shrugs, "so don't worry."

Cole rests his head back against his seat, staring

up at the sky full of stars. He hopes to hell Tim isn't one for sleeping in, because come seven a.m. they are raiding the motherfucking house.

***

Savannah

I move my head side to side, tuning in and out of someone speaking.

"Do you think it was wise to mention Roth to her?" Tim's voice seems far away.

A ticking sound makes my stomach turn. I know he's here; his damn boots give him away.

"Are you questioning my motives?" His voice makes my blood freeze in place. "She needs to know that her life is over, that she can be reborn again with me. I never gave his name, never said how close he's getting to—" I can't hold on. I feel myself slipping back into a place that makes me feel no pain, only love.

Three hours later I am in agony. I cry out as the American slaps me and then punches me in the stomach for the second time. My mouth is getting me in trouble again. I know it would be better for me if I kept quiet, but I'd rather make him angry and be hit than be forced to sleep with this man.

"You will bend to my ways, Savannah," he barks down at me as his stupid cobra boots tap along the wooden floor. For the last hour he has been questioning me, trying to gain some information on where Tim went. He had heard from one of the girls that Tim had spent some time in my room when I arrived. I wasn't about to out the one person who may be helping me. "Did you sleep with him, Savannah? I should have known you were a little slut. You probably spread your legs for the whole damn Army." I smirk at him, thinking that if he suspects I slept with his muscle that maybe he won't touch me. "You think this is funny?"

"No." I slowly shake my head, feeling lightheaded with pain. "I think it's hysterical. You wanted me so badly that you hunted me down for so long, and five minutes with Tim and he's got me against the wall doing the one thing you've been fantasizing about for all that time?" Well, that was it. I found The American's weak spot. His eyes widen as red hot anger flickers across them. I see him lose all sense of control. Oh, shit.

I curl up in a ball, my knees protecting my stomach and my arms covering my head, and hold on. This beating takes me to the edge, and I know it could be the end. I force my thoughts to turn inward, ignoring the punishment my body is taking.

I'm twelve, sitting on my bed and clipping pictures from a magazine. My mother comes in my room holding two cups of lemonade. She's so weak she can barely hold their weight, so I hop up and take them from her, then clear a spot on my bed for her to sit. She leans over to see what I'm doing. I return to gluing the pictures on the Bristol board, telling her it's my art project for family studies. We have to show what our perfect apartment would look like.

"I love the colors." She smiles, pointing at the

red couch and matching red appliances. I try not to stare at her for too long. She gets uncomfortable with how much weight she has lost. She has commented on her own reflection and old she looks. She has taken to wearing silk scarves around her neck in pretty colors. I think she still looks beautiful, even when she's just wearing her head scarf and not her wig. My mother could walk around bald and still be the most gorgeous woman in the room. "You know, when I was eighteen, my best friend Jessi and I got a place together. It wasn't much, but we had been saving for two summers and we went out and bought everything new. I remember I bought a red Mixmaster. It cost me a lot, but it was the absolute favorite of all that I got that day. I loved that mixer. I had so much fun experimenting with recipes. It's how I started making those chocolate chip cookies you love so much."

"Oh, so that's the story of how your famous cookies came about. Well, in that case..." I reach behind me and hold up a red Mixmaster picture and glue it on my counter. "Now my apartment is perfect."

She reaches out and runs her soft hand along my cheek. "Promise me someday when you get your own place you'll live for both of us." I want to burst into tears. I hate when my mom talks like this, but it's the truth, it's our reality, and my mother who I love more than anything is dying a slow, painful death. And every day she is here trying to be strong for me and my father, a father who is rarely home anymore. "All I ask from you, Savi, is to live it to the fullest and be happy. Do it for me, if not for yourself."

"I promise," I whisper, fighting the tears.

"You can cry, honey. I cry too." She lets go and starts to tear up along with me. *"It's okay not to be strong. Part of living is feeling, and part of feeling is hurting."* I move to crawl up next to her. *"As long as you don't let the hurt consume you. Sometimes we all just need time to work it out."*

"I don't want you to leave me, Mom." I sob into her t-shirt. *"I don't know what to do without you."*

She holds me as tight as she can. *"Just because you can't see me, doesn't mean I'm not here, Savannah, and you're half of me, so therefore I'm never really gone."*

A sharp kick to my battered ribs jolts me back to reality. I'm flooded with incredible pain and everything goes black as I pass out again. This time my mom is nowhere to be found, only darkness and pain and loss. Once again I am alone.

"Up." His voice breaks my lovely dream.

My mother starts to fade, and the last thing I hear her say is, *"Fight, my sweet Savannah, fight for your life."* Sunlight burns through the holes in the roof, making me squint. I see The American is wearing nothing but a pair of satin PJ pants.

Oh no.

He reaches down and undoes my handcuffs, scooping me in his arms and holding me close to his chest. His lips make contact with my hair and I force my tongue back. "How badly did I hurt you?"

Are you fucking kidding me? Is this a joke?

He walks me out of the attic, down the stairs, and through a hallway I don't recognize. The lights are dim, the smell of flowers fills my nose, and faint music can be heard as we approach an open door. I catch the blonde girl from dinner peek out the door at me. Her eyes fill with tears as she steps back in the darkness.

"I want to make you feel better, Savannah." His voice is low and in control, not like earlier. "This is my room," he says as he steps across the threshold.

Oh my hell.

A king-size bed sits in the middle of a large room. Brown curtains with gold patterns hang heavy throughout the space. A fireplace is lit, and a record player is playing an old Louisiana tune. Candles hang off the wall on dungeon-looking holders. I do spot another pair of handcuffs dangling from the headboard.

I thought I was past feeling fear, thought I'd seen it all.

He places me on the bed. "Now, my love, time to use your mouth in the way it's intended. Lean back and open up."

No. I was wrong. This is my deepest, darkest fear.

***

Cole

Cole checks his watch once again. Every minute that ticks by makes him grow more and more angry. All he can think of is that while this fat fucker sleeps in a warm bed, Savannah is chained to a wall. He senses Mark's mood is the same. All it takes is one look at him and they both slip out of the SUV with their weapons raised.

"I was wondering how much longer," Keith smirks as the rest exit the SUV.

It's nearly four thirty in the morning, and darkness surrounds the house. The team moves as if they are part of the night. Cole takes a quick inventory of how many are in the house, and they confirm six. Tim Powers, his three men, the mother, and younger woman.

Daniel moves smoothly as he picks the lock and opens the door for John and Paul to move in. The two brothers are passed out on the couch. Cole and Mark move into the bedroom Tim and the younger woman are in. Cole nods to Mark as he points a gun at the woman's head. Cole wraps his gloved hand over Tim's mouth and nudges his rifle hard into his side. Tim's eyes pop open. He starts to move but stops when he realizes what's happening. Cole tells him to keep quiet and points to the girl with a gun to her head. Tim nods that he understands.

"Good. Now get up and walk outside. Our men have everyone in this place covered. We have plenty of firepower, so keep your mouth shut. You try anything, and they all die."

"Yeah," Tim shakes his head, then Cole pulls him to his feet and shoves him out the door. Tim moves through the living room, taking in the fact that Paul and John have guns pointed at his friends. Once outside, they hurry him to the SUV. They cuff him, pat him down, and then push him into the truck. A steel divider separates the back from the rest of the vehicle, so Daniel keeps a gun pointed on Tim as they speed away from the house. Within minutes they're on the road heading to an open field they saw earlier.

Pulling off the road, Mark hops out and opens the back of the truck, grabbing Tim and slamming him to the ground. The men point their weapons at his face. Green lasers bounce around on his chest. Cole pulls out his flashlight and shines it in his face, making him look away.

"I take it you're here for the girl?" Tim grunts, shifting his body in obvious discomfort on the rocky soil. "I was waiting for you."

"So here we are; now where's the girl?" Cole asks calmly.

"The American has her," he answers, pissing off Cole. He wants a damn location, not the name of the shit he already knows.

Cole grabs his shirt and sends a powerful punch into his face, breaking his nose. *Fuck that feels good.* Tim shouts and slumps forward, hitting his head on the ground. Mark pulls him back to a kneeling position.

"I repeat, where is the girl?"

Tim spits blood on the ground, breathing hard. "I was helping her, man, I was going to get her back to you."

"Bullshit." Cole pulls his arm back and glances at Mark. "Kill the brothers." Mark starts to turn, but Tim shouts for him to stop.

"Please! Don't!" He curses and squeezes his eyes shut for a moment. "Denton has her at his place."

Shattered

Cole slowly lowers his hand, waiting for him to go on. "Denton, The American, he has her. *Mierda*! I'm not lying. He has her, he has many girls in the house. I can take you to him. She is in the attic, her mouth got her in trouble, so..." Tim lifts his shoulders in an exaggerated shrug. "I can show you where, but don't hurt my family. My brothers may be *hombres estupidos*, but they're all I've got."

"Girl first." Cole nods to John, who shoves Tim into the middle row of the SUV. Cole calls Mike back at Shadows and fills him in on everything, including The American's proper name. Mike has arranged for a chopper to be standing by, ready for the pickup. Mike tells Cole that he has established contact with a few Mexican police, friends of a friend, willing to provide support with the mission and to take out The American if need be. Nothing would please Cole more than to kill The American, but they need him alive. They have questions on so many other kidnappings that only he can answer.

They drive for forty minutes down a long desert road, and Cole knows the sun will be up in an hour. Time is running out. Normally they'd wait until that night, but there's no way he's making Savannah stay in that place for any longer than she has to. Cole speaks to the team in French, letting them know how the attack will play out.

"See that light up there?" Tim points to it with his chin since his hands are cuffed behind him. "That's the house. Denton will either be in the attic with your girlfriend or in his bedroom in the back."

Cole leans forward to get a better view of the grounds as they get closer. John pulls off to the side of the road, pulling on his night vision goggles, as do the rest of the men. John starts asking Tim about the security system and any triggers around the property. Tim fills them in, but they all take it with a grain of salt.

Finally, after sending the coordinates to Mike, they head on foot toward the house.

Cole signals to his father and Keith to take the west, and to Paul and John to take the north side of the property with Tim. Mark nods to Cole as they sneak up behind one man and his dog. Mark tosses a rock in the opposite direction, throwing the dog off while he wraps a rag around the animal's mouth, making him fall fast asleep. Cole's arm slips around the man's neck, snapping it without hesitation. Mark lowers the dog carefully to the ground and gives him a quick pat.

Moving on, they encounter three more men, killing them instantly. Before they hear the panting, they see the flash of color leap in the air and grab Mark's arm, sinking its teeth into his flesh. Mark jams his gun in between its jaws, breaking its hold. The dog whimpers as he runs off toward the house.

"You good?" Cole asks, scanning for their next victim.

"The bitch bites me, and *he* has the nerve to cry. What the fuck?" Mark hisses, wrapping his wound. "Why can't people have cats? Really, all they do is sit there and plot your death…is that so bad?"

Cole chuckles as he shifts positions, happy to hear Mark is indeed all right. "Remember that the next time you're cursing Scoot for getting your pants full of fur."

Shattered

"Love the furry prick," Mark huffs.

A snap from behind them has Cole pointing his laser beam at his father's head. "The west side is a no go." Daniel nods to Keith coming up next to him. "I say we enter through the north door, keep a low profile, grab Savi, and get the fuck out."

They quickly hatch a new plan, fill Paul and John in on it, and hurry to make their move before the sun starts to rise.

"Watch your step." Keith points out two triggers that will set the house alarm off if you step on them. "They're scattered throughout the property." Cole nods, taking note. It makes him wonder how many of The American's men set off the alarm in the past.

"Those triggers are the least of your worries," Tim butts in, getting a hit to the gut with a rifle by Keith. "I'm just saying there are too many men for you all to take out."

"We'll see," Cole grunts.

Weaving in and out of the triggers, the men keep on high alert.

When they're about five yards away from the door, a click echoes through the morning air. Everyone freezes. Cole slowly turns to see John's scrunched-up face.

"Fuck me," John growls and glances down at his right shoe, which is holding down the trigger.

"Don't move," Cole whispers, waiting for the attack. But nothing happens.

"If you lift your foot," Daniel says calmly, "it will trip the alarm."

"Go." John flicks his head. "Let me know when you're on your way out, and I'll book it back to the car."

"No—" Paul cuts him off, looking over at Cole. "You guys got this?"

Cole nods, knowing he'd never leave Mark unprotected either. "I'll let you know. Stay low."

Daniel makes it to the porch first, scanning the wood for triggers. He signals all is safe. "Set your watches. We're in and out in ten minutes."

"Where's the bedroom from here?" Keith shoves Tim to the stairs, making sure he knows who's in charge. "Speak."

"Stairs will be right there." Tim flexes his shoulders like the handcuffs are too tight, trying to point to the entryway. "At the end of the hall there's a set of double doors, that's Denton's room. More than likely she's there."

"You better be right." Keith looks over at Cole, who is ticking with anger.

Cole glances over his shoulder one last time at his guys before they disappear into the house.

One of the female servants freezes as she watches the men enter the house.

"The new girl?" Cole hisses in a whisper. The woman mouths master bedroom in Spanish. Cole's stomach drops. "Not a word," he whispers back.

She nods then holds up a hand. "The others, please," she pushes her hands together like she's praying, "let them go." Daniel nods from Cole's left.

"Move." Cole jams the gun a little harder into Tim's back.

"Hey!" someone yells from another room. Keith is quick, popping two bullets into his forehead. The woman who just helped them cups her mouth to stop her scream. Suddenly she points behind them just as another guy tries to stab Daniel. Cole kicks his knee, forcing it to snap in the wrong direction. He takes the butt of the gun and rams it into the man's temple.

"Move." Cole can tell things are escalating quickly.

They slowly move up the stairs. The first room to the left is open...strange when every other door is closed, so Daniel does a quick sweep then signals the all clear.

"It's your girl's room," Tim whispers to Cole, before moving forward down the hallway. Cole watches the bottom of each door in case any lights turn on; they need to stay invisible. "The master is at the end of the hall with the double doors. I knock twice so he knows it's me."

Cole leads the pack. He looks at the men as they approach. Tension is high, to say the least. He nods at Tim, who lifts his sweaty fist and knocks twice.

"Tim, that fucking better be you!" The American shouts, his voice a high pitched squeal. "You better have done what I asked!"

Tim opens the door and moves inside, smiling. "Yeah, Denton, not only did I get the Colonel, I got his whole fucking ar—"

Trap...it's a fucking trap! So many things are happening in front of Cole, but nothing matters when he knocks Tim to the floor and catches sight of why The American is so panicky.

No...

Chapter Eleven

The American is straddling Savannah's lifeless body, giving her CPR. One look at the guns drawn and he jumps back, raising his hands.

Daniel is the first to move. He races forward, hitting The American with the butt of his gun. Shrieks become louder as two females burst out of the bathroom and attack Keith and Mark.

Cole leaps forward, climbing on top of Savannah. Two fingers check her pulse while his other hand checks her pupils. "Please, baby," he whispers. Shutting out the war around him, he concentrates on trying to bring life back to her body. Nothing. He shoots up, lacing his fingers on top of one another pumping her chest, desperately wishing he could reach inside her and hold her heart in his hands. One, two, three...he counts, his lips meet with hers and fill her lungs with his own breath. Focusing all his energy on her, he's hoping for a miracle. She looks so small and fragile, her beautiful eyes once so lit with fire are cold and dim. "Don't you dare leave me, Savannah. I swear to god

I will give you the world if you come back to me."

Mark suddenly appears at his side, his hands moving all around as he tries to assess the scene. "Mark." Cole's voice breaks as he looks at his brother in pain.

"Come on, Savi." Mark starts rubbing her limp arm. "We need you."

"Please, no!" Cole begs. His *everything* is slipping away, the only woman he's ever loved, the mother of his unborn baby, leaving him, but not by choice. Damn it, it's not fair! He pounds on her tiny chest, feeling the world has committed the worst crime…there is no good on this earth …only evil.

Suddenly, Savannah gasps and starts coughing, twisting to her side under him. "Savi!" Cole shouts, grabbing her head and pulling her to him. She starts sobbing, and a horrible shaking takes her, her breath ragged. He carefully strokes her back and watches her blue-tinged face slowly turn to a waxy white. As soon as she takes him in, she whispers his name. He wraps her in his arms gently, allowing himself a moment to breathe.

"Cole." Mark's voice gets through to him.

Snapping out of it and back into Army mode, Cole realizes they don't have much time before company arrives. He pushes the fear of the last several minutes away to deal with later, knowing right now he needs to get them all out of here alive. Keith informs them that one of the girls tripped the alarm. Paul and John are now guarding the door, waiting for them to arrive. The redhead in question is looking at them with a nasty expression on her face. Damn, it won't be long. They have to get out now. Cole looks at the girls and tells them if they want their freedom they better get the hell out now. The blonde girl eyes Savannah's trembling body then bolts down the hallway, but the rest stand in fear or, God knows, they might be suffering from a type of Stockholm syndrome or something. Either way, he figures he isn't going to worry about them; they aren't his problem. "Let's move!" he directs his men. Daniel and Mark force a handcuffed Tim and The American to their feet and head down the hallway.

"Raven One to Fox Two," John's voice flows over the radio, "we've got company in five minutes." Gunshots ring over their earpieces. "You guys need to move now!"

"Ten-four," Mark answers. "Get the SUV ready, we're transferring two hostages."

"Copy that, Fox Two."

John and Paul spray bullets at the men as they try and close in on them. They take out more than half of The American's army. The rest seem to pull back when they get sight of Blackstone's hostages.

Daniel has the two men blindfolded and piles them in the truck, handcuffing them to a metal bar. Tim is pleading with Daniel to let him go, that it was all a misunderstanding, while The American remains silent.

Cole feels Savannah's grip tighten as he gets closer to the vehicle. He wishes he planned this better as he jumps inside, keeping her on his lap tight against his chest. Mark, Daniel, and Keith squeeze in beside them, while Paul takes the front with John.

Shattered

"Call it in," Cole orders Paul once they are on the road. Headlights are coming up quickly behind them.

Savannah doesn't speak. She barely even moves. He has to keep shifting to make sure she is all right. Her eyes are glued to Daniel's watch, and she hardly blinks. It takes everything Cole has not to turn around and kill the man who tried to take everything from him. Wanting answers on what the fuck happened back at the house is eating away at his mind.

Ten, fifteen, twenty minutes go by. Cole keeps checking the side mirror, watching the same headlights follow them along the dark road. No shots have been fired yet.

"I can smell you, my love," The American whispers into the silence, making Savannah tense as she hears his voice, snapping her out of her trance. Daniel shakes his head at Cole, making sure he doesn't react. "I can still feel your soft lips, your smooth skin, and the taste of your tongue." Savannah turns her face into Cole's chest, silently sobbing.

"He's trying to get to you, baby, just tune him out," Cole whispers in her ear. He kisses her softly, wanting to calm her.

The American chuckles and leans his head back against the window. "When my hands felt that last tiny gasp of air pass through your lungs, I knew I should've stopped, but your eyes were hypnotic. You held me in the moment."

Cole reaches forward and grabs Paul's stun gun from his hip. He shifts Savannah so she is sitting upright, turns, and forces the tip of the gun through the bars and stuns The American in the neck before anyone has time to react. The American screams out, his body jolting upward. "One more word and I'll kill you." Cole doesn't even recognize his own voice he's so fucking livid. Yanking the wires from the gun, he presses Savannah back down to his chest and hands the gun to his father while the asshole tries to control his breathing.

"House to Blackstone," Mike's voice breaks through.

Cole presses the button on his neck to activate his earpiece. "Go ahead."

"Chopper is standing by, backup arriving in five, Frank and Eagle Eye will meet you on the other side of the border. We see you on satellite and are monitoring behind you, will communicate if they show signs of making a move. So far they're only watching."

"Copy that."

***

Savannah

I squeeze my eyes shut, concentrating on Cole's smell, sweat mixed with soap. It's just what I need to ground me. So much has happened it's hard to stay focused. I'm tired, sore, my neck and throat feel like they're on fire, and my head is pounding. It's terrifying to know The American, Denton, or whatever his name is, is sitting a foot away from me. He tried to kill me and almost succeeded. My mind goes to Tim. He was using me; thank god that backfired. But am I really safe? This will never really be over until The American is dead. I don't even realize what I am doing until I feel Cole's hand slip on top of mine, stopping me from taking his gun from his leg holster. Instead of saying anything, he laces his fingers through mine, ever so calmly bringing them to rest on my leg. His lips kiss my hair for a long minute, breathing in deeply and helping me drift off to an unpleasant sleep.

Suddenly all hell breaks loose and I'm being hoisted out of the car. I'm in Mark's arms now, not Cole's, and there is a lot of shouting, gunshots, and a chopper whose rotor is madly cutting into the early morning air. My brain fights to catch up with this madness.

"Move, move, move!" someone shouts at Mark. Paul is shooting off to our left. I can see the concentration on his face and the puffs of dust as bullets ping around him. It all comes at me as if in slow motion. I see John inside the chopper with his hand extended, reaching out for me. His mouth is moving as though he is yelling something. I can feel the jolt of each step Mark takes as he runs toward John. I feel no pain now; it's all so surreal. When we are close enough, I'm tossed into John's arms and he lifts me into the chopper. He places me on a seat across from The American, who is still bound and blindfolded. I scan about the massive chopper and can't find Cole.

The pilot is shouting for the guys to get in, and John is barking out orders to Paul, who is still firing off his weapon. Mark suddenly flies inside with

Daniel, who looks to be bleeding from his arm. The chopper blades are kicking up a huge dust storm, making it hard to see and hear the fight outside. I feel the chopper start to shift. *What's going on?* Cole and Keith jump on at the last moment before we rise into the sky, and my body sags with relief.

I can't keep my eyes away from The American. It's odd seeing him looking so vulnerable. With his handcuffs and blindfold, he certainly doesn't frighten me anymore. He's not wearing his stupid cobra boots. He's barefoot, wearing only a pair of jeans and a shirt. Memories flood through me of him on top of me in the bedroom, of the lies Tim told me that if I cried he'd stay away, knowing now that only made him more intrigued. I feel sick as I think of it. The harder I sobbed, the harder he squeezed the life out of me. I stopped fighting him. I would rather be dead than give in to that man and let him have me.

I reach into the top of my dress and slowly ease out the tiny blade from my bra. Looking around, I see that everyone looks exhausted. Cole is wrapping Daniel's arm, and the others' attention is on that. As much as my body hurts, as much as I'm mentally finished and just want to close my eyes again, I know this might be my only chance.

I shift silently onto my knees and crawl forward. I catch Keith's face as my movement draws his gaze, but he doesn't stop me. He's just watching. He puts a hand on Mark when he turns my way. It's not easy moving around on the chopper, but I make the five foot distance and sit on my knees next to The American. Leaning in and letting my hair brush his shoulder, he senses my presence and his face turns up with a smile. My lips are close to his ear as I whisper so only he can hear me.

"Anyone can be bought, Denton. It's all about finding their weakness. Yours was me. Problem is I already belong to someone else, and that someone else always gets what's his. You never had me, and you never will. So while you sit in your six by twelve jail cell I want you to picture the Colonel with his hands on my body, touching me, and my moans of ecstasy that are his alone."

His neck muscles flex as he clamps down on his jaw. "This will never end, my love." He suddenly leans into me. Even through his blindfold I can feel his eyes burning into mine. "I always win." His mouth is still smiling at me.

He's right. I'll never be free if I don't end this now. My eyes drop down to his long throat, and the blade in my hand becomes hot as fire. As I raise my arm, I see my future flash in front of me. If this doesn't end, I'll forever be afraid. All my anger boils to the surface as I throw my body weight forward, aiming for his neck. A large hand wraps around my wrist while the other hooks my waist and pulls me to the other side of the chopper.

"It's what he wants, Savi," Cole huffs in my ear. "He wants you to kill him. His hell is being caught. Let him live so he can suffer." He pries the blade from my fingers and hands it to Keith, who is shaking his head with a smirk like I never stop surprising him. "It's over, Savannah, I promise it's over."

***

We make two stops before we finally land back in Montana at the safe house. The American, whose name I now know is Denton, is handed off to Frank and a team of his men who arrived back from TJ just hours earlier. Daniel had to be dropped off at a private hospital in North Dakota to have his wound treated. When I ask what happened to Tim, The American's muscle, Keith tells me he got shot in the head. I nod, not wanting to know which team did the deed, since I now know Tim's loyalty lay with Denton all along. He used me to try and trap Cole into coming to the market. Thank god Cole was smart enough to see through it. I hate that I didn't.

Stepping down on solid ground and taking in the scenery feels pretty amazing, but seeing Abigail and June run up and wrap me in a bear hug is even better. Thinking back, I know there was a point I didn't think I was going to be here again. I thought I was going to live the rest of my crazy, messed up life with Denton or until I made it end. As they fuss over me, I feel a bubble of warmth start to rise from my stomach to my heart.

"Come on, dear, you must be freezing!" I tug Cole's jacket around me a little tighter as she looks at my bare legs in the army boots, smiling. "Let's get you inside." I glance back at Cole, seeing him smile and nod at me. I return the smile, but it fades when I start to walk, as the soreness in my body reminds me of what The American did to me physically.

Sitting in my room on the edge of my bed, I'm

Shattered

still huddled under Cole's jacket, wanting to shake off an odd feeling that has a grip on me. I know I'm terribly tired and I want a shower, but I can't bring myself to move. I wonder where my father and Lynn are. I wonder what they're doing right now and if they've heard that I'm free again. I feel my face prickle all over like I want to cry, but I don't. I just sit and stare at the floor.

I may have fallen asleep for a few minutes, because I find myself slumped on the bed uncomfortably. I finally force myself up and get showered, dressed, and back downstairs to find everyone doing what they do best whenever they come from back from a job. Drinks in the living room. It feels wonderful to be back here, and I find myself thinking of Derek, realizing I'll never see him again. I want to mourn for him, knowing that it is my fault he's not with us, my fault he's being buried, and why his little niece won't be getting her New York snow globe. I got him killed; that death is on me, and me alone.

"One Marcus Martini for you." Mark grins as his eyes fall to my neck where I know from checking myself out in the bathroom mirror I have a purple and blue necklace of bruises. I gladly take the drink and pluck an olive off the stick. "Cole should be down soon, he's just making his report. Look, Savi, I know you've been through a lot. I hope you know how much we all care about you. Is there anything you want to talk about? Are you okay?"

"That's a big question," I answer honestly.

Mark nods, looking at the room full of all our friends smiling and talking. "This is a big day, not only because we brought you back home, Savi, but we took down The American. It's been a long seven-year hunt for that bastard. He's been a real thorn in our side, and every one of these guys has reason to celebrate."

I tuck my feelings aside and click Mark's beer. "You're right, Mark. You know I love you guys and couldn't be more thankful for what you've all done for me. Now let's go celebrate."

Later that night, I lie back on my pillow and think about the evening. Cole wasn't able to come celebrate at all in the end, as he had a video conference with Frank and some other important people about the capture of The American. I am too tired to last more than a few hours and really just want to sleep and turn off for a while. *Thinking is overrated.*

It is about three a.m. when I feel Cole slip into bed with me. Something cold touches my skin, and I feel him placing my snowflake chain back on, fastening it around my neck. I squeeze my eyes shut, realizing how much I missed its comfort. His arm slides over me and pulls my back flush against his front. He sighs and breathes me in deeply then tucks his face into my neck, lacing my fingers with his, and we both fall into a deep sleep.

***

The week goes by in an odd blur. Everyone seems to be doing their thing, whereas I just float around unable to focus on anything. Cole is extremely busy. I've seen him twice for dinner, but he doesn't talk much and seems preoccupied. His apologetic comment that he is mentally fried was given with a quick hug in the hallway. Abigail and June are helping Derek's sister with his funeral arrangements but don't talk to me about it. I'm sure they are only being kind, but leaving me out of it makes me feel isolated and guilty instead. Keith, John, and Paul are hardly around, and Mike only will talk to me if I stray too far off the grounds.

I start to feel strange in this house, a little lost and, frankly, a little hurt. No, to be honest, I'm really hurting. Feeling my mood sink even lower, my heart weighs heavily in my chest. I find myself drawn down to the entertainment room. Sliding down onto the smooth wooden bench, my fingers lift the cover, exposing the soothing ivory keys.

My eyes close and my heart swells as I feel her sit down next to me. Letting out a long, slow breath, my fingers touch the keys softly.

"Let's play our song, but add a little of your flavor to it," Mom suggests, grinning at me with a bump to the shoulder. "Come on, sweetie, let whatever is bothering you flow out through your fingers." I take in a another deep breath and let the pain flow from my soul.

The first line to *These Arms of Mine* by Otis Redding slips past my lips, and the notes start to form the song's beautiful melody.

***

Cole

Cole moves about the kitchen looking for something quick to eat, but nothing looks appetizing. Abigail joins him, holding a newspaper which she drops on the counter in front of him. Cole leans forward and reads the headlines, seeing the news about The American has made the front page. "One of America's most wanted fugitives captured."

"The question is will her father be next?" Abigail sets a sandwich down in front of him. "You need to eat more than an apple. I can make myself another one. Where's Savi? I haven't seen much of her lately."

"You don't hear that?" Mark says as he snatches the sandwich off the plate and takes three big bites. Cole steps out into the living room, hearing the piano and Savannah's deep, soulful voice. He turns to look at Mark in disbelief. "Yeah, for like ten minutes now. Girl has some mad talent."

Before he gets a chance to hear much more, the song ends. The sound of the piano cover closing has Cole and Abigail slipping back into the kitchen, pretending to be busy as Savannah climbs the stairs and enters the room. She blushes slightly as she sees them. He can tell she thought she was alone in this part of the house.

"Hey, Savi," Abigail says, standing in front of the fridge. "You thirsty? I just made some lemonade."

She nods and comes over to the island, standing next to Cole. He leans over and gives her a kiss on

Shattered

the cheek, but her body turns slightly, almost as though she doesn't want it. "Are you all right?" Her body language screams no, but she nods.

"Really, Savi?" Mark says through a mouthful of cookie. "You're gonna lie to Logan?" he sputters, sending crumbs into the air. "You seem to forget what we do for a living. Besides, the way you played and sang that song nearly brought me to my knees in tears."

"Mark!" Abigail scowls, making Savannah gasp. "Filter, my son," she scolds him.

"What?" He shrugs. "It was a compliment."

***

Savannah

I shift while watching him scribble on his tablet. Snow is falling outside the window behind him, brightening up all the scruffy areas, softening the landscape in a winter wonderland again. "Tell me, Savannah, how does it feel to be back?" Dr. Roberts asks, as we sip our coffee in our usual meeting room next to Cole's office. I was the one who asked him to come this morning. Something feels off, and I want to get to the bottom of it.

"It feels great…good, I mean. It's a relief to be back, of course."

"But…" He pulls his glasses down on his nose, knowing there's more.

I shrug, not sure how to put it. "I don't know. I mean, I've been back here for a week now. I'm happy. I'm safe. I'm so grateful to the guys…I just thought it would feel a little different."

"How different?"

I shift again and tuck my dress a little tighter around my legs, feeling nervous about answering this question, knowing that once I say it out loud, it makes it true. "It feels like it's not quite where I need to be."

He nods like he understands me instead of displaying the confusion I expected from him. "Savannah, you were left to look after your mother for the four years she was ill. Weren't you fourteen when she passed?" I nod miserably. "So, that would have made you ten when you took on a very adult emotional task, correct?" I nod, agreeing. "Okay, so then after your mother died, your father began his political climb to the mayor's office, thrusting you into his world. Suddenly the press is hounding you, your life is turned upside down, and you start to run into problems, so you put your life on hold once again for your parents. A few years later you are kidnapped and held for seven terrible months." I clear my throat uncomfortably and start to say something, but he holds up his hand and continues. "Finally, you are rescued and brought here. Then," he pauses with his finger in the air, "a few months later you are taken once again, then rescued *and* brought back here again." He looks at me with one eyebrow raised, waiting for a response.

"Okay…" is all I can muster.

"What I'm saying, Savannah, is you need to give yourself some time for you. You need to process all that has happened. You haven't had a chance to live your *own* life yet. You're twenty-nine years old and—"

"...Still feel like I'm going in circles with no direction and no end in sight," I answer, feeling like he has just hit the source of my problem. "I don't really know who I am and what I want, and now that all my major life-altering problems seem to be ending, I find myself lost." A horrible feeling hits my stomach when I suddenly think of Cole.

"Finding yourself doesn't mean you have to give up anything. It just means you need a little time to be alone."

"Space," I whisper, closing my eyes. "I think I just need some space that's mine."

***

Cole

Cole hangs up the phone after a long three-hour conversation with Frank. Turns out they have enough evidence to convict Lynn, thanks to Joe Might, who is willing to throw her under the bus to get a lesser sentence for himself. However, the Mayor is pinning it all on Luka Donavan. It's easier to blame the dead than the living who have a voice.

He pours himself a cup of coffee and leans against the window, watching the snow fall. A storm is coming. They're supposed to be getting forty-five inches of snow. He's thankful his father arrived home safely last night. A bullet grazed his shoulder, and now he and Mark are joking that they actually planned their new matching scars.

"Cole?" Savannah whispers behind him. He

turns, feeling the strange vibe that seems to be there whenever they are together lately. He knows he really needs to address the Derek issue, as she still must have raw feelings about it. She's been acting different since she got back, and it's not like her to keep him at arm's length. It's killing him. "Cole," she repeats when he doesn't answer right away, "do you have a moment?"

He nods and rubs his face. God, he is tired. He sits down on the couch while she takes a seat across from him.

"Why?" he asks without thinking.

"Why what?"

"Why are you over there and not over here next to me?"

"Because I don't think clearly when I'm that close to you."

"Well, I don't like it," he admits.

She stares at him for a moment then comes over and sits next to him. His hand reaches for her automatically, tugging her closer, but she stops him. She slides to the other end of the couch, looking uncomfortable.

"Okay, I'm listening," he says, raising his hand to show her he won't grab for her again.

It takes her a few minutes, but she finally clears her throat. "I saw some pictures."

He doesn't hesitate. "Savannah, we met Jose four months ago. He thought we were looking for work with The Cartels. The guy is a bit of an idiot, and we quickly gained intel on your whereabouts. We met up with him a few times at that café, and apparently so did The American. That's how we found you—"

"No," she interrupts, her face growing pale, "not that picture."

Cole turns, pulling a leg up so he can look at her better. "Then which?"

"The one with the blonde." His stomach rolls. *Oh fuck,* how the hell? "The one where you were holding her in your arms like you hold me. The one where you are staring at her with the same look you have for me. The one where you are kissing her with the same lips you use on me." She pauses, nearly in tears. "I thought…" She shakes her head, standing and putting more distance between them. "I'm sure there's some reason why you were doing that with her, but…"

"There is," he chimes in.

She holds up her hand to stop him. "But regardless, those little things mean something to me. I thought they were *only* for me."

"They are." He stands and goes to her, but she steps back. He hates not being able to touch her when he wants to. He shouldn't, but he shares, "She's an informant for Shadows. She's the one who helps us gain info on the Cartel. Her brother runs tight with them. She's had a crush on me forever, and when you were taken, I knew I had to…I played dirty to get anything I could on your whereabouts. But, Savannah, she means nothing to me. I did it all for you, for us." He can feel her pull away mentally, her big beautiful eyes filling with tears again. "I love you, Savannah, I always have. Please don't pull away from me. My heart can't take losing you again."

She steps forward, then stops as big, silent tears roll down her cheeks. With each one that falls, a piece of his own heart falls along with it. "I promised Keith I'd help him with something."

"Savannah, please." Cole catches her by the hand, but she shakes her head, making him release her immediately.

As she reaches the door, she turns, keeping her head down. "I love you, Cole, but put yourself in my shoes. Think about how much that would hurt seeing me with another man, looking at him like that, even if it *was* for a good reason."

"It would destroy me," he admits, feeling sick.

She nods once, then slowly closes the door behind her.

Cole grabs for one of his brandy glasses and sends it across the room, feeling all kinds of fucked up emotions. It shatters into a million pieces right along with his heart.

Chapter Twelve

Savannah

Walking, walking, and more walking around half of the lake, I'm just trying to make sense of everything. By the time I make it back to the house, I'm more mixed up than I was when I started. It's late, the sun is setting, and the snow is coming down harder. After a quick trip to my room, I go to the kitchen, grab a bottle of wine, a glass, and an opener, and head downstairs. Luckily, most of the guys have been busy with the wind-up of The American case, so everyone seems to be keeping to themselves.

I step out into the freezing air in a pair of flips flops. Climbing up onto a chair, I cover the camera pointing in my direction with a t-shirt. I rip off my top and chuck my shorts to the side. I toss my hair into a messy bun as I sink into the deliciously hot water. It feels divine. I instantly feel the tension slip away from my body. In the winter they keep the hot tub covered with a tent that opens at the sides. I open only one flap, so I have a private view of the lake.

My second glass in, and I feel pretty damn relaxed. I can't believe I haven't come here sooner. Closing my eyes, leaning my head back, I listen to how quiet the snow makes everything. It makes for a perfect moment.

"See, Savi, this is the perfect place for a vacation." Lynn grins with a lime green straw wedged between her lips. She's on her fourth margarita since we hit the beach an hour ago. She surprised me with a trip to Fiji for my birthday. We're staying in a little bungalow on Castaway Island. No one knows me, allowing me to blend in perfectly.

I slip my sunglasses on, plucking the melon from the rim of my mojito and popping it in my mouth. The cold juice is refreshing. "Yes." A grin tugs at my lips, as our morning yoga trainer, Diogo, grabs a paddle board and heads for the crisp blue ocean. "I think this is one of the best presents you've ever given me."

She laughs, clinking her drink to mine. He might be married, but nothing matters with an ass like that.

"I wonder where his tan line ends." I give her a devilish grin.

She shakes her head. "I have goggles, wanna go find out?"

"Yup!"

A shadow casts over Lynn, making me squint to see who's interrupting our fun.

Shattered

"Hello, ladies, my name is Jerry. I teach a scuba class with the resort." Jerry grins with a large set of pearly whites and shows us his hotel ID. *"Our first class starts in ten. Would you like to join?"*

I glance at Lynn, who is downing her drink with a dirty grin.

"Yes, Jerry, that sounds like a great plan."

Poor Diogo.

I didn't even know I was grinning until my reality comes crashing around me, making my eyes pop open. I rub a spot over my heart, which hurts like hell when I think of our happy *fake* memories. I wonder if my father planned the whole trip, just to get me out of the media.

"I hate my past," I bitch, shaking Lynn's face from my thoughts.

"I'm glad I didn't send Dell out here to check on the camera," Cole says, standing in front of the open side and making me jump. His hands are tucked into his pockets as snowflakes hit then disappear when they meet the heat of his body through his sweater. He's very sexy in his black sweater and jeans. "Is that even considered a bikini?" I think about my suit rather than look at it. I guess its white strings may be a little skimpy, but I wasn't planning on having company. "You want to be left alone?" I shake my head and take a slow sip of my wine, watching him intently. He yanks off his sweater, giving me a moment to gawk at his strong arms, chest, and back. I try to hide my body's natural reaction to him, but it's impossible. Pure lust rises to the surface whenever he's around. His pants come off next and are set down carefully by his boots, his inner Army ways coming out. He settles in the water across from me, his legs stretched out on either side. Our eyes wander over one another, both knowing we've been physically attracted to each other from day one, so neither of us even pretends to look away.

I tip my glass of wine in his direction as if to ask if he wants some. He nods, holding out a hand for me to come to him, but first I lean back and pour more wine into my glass. Keeping low in the water, my eyes on his, I move toward him, stopping just in front of him but not quite touching. He suddenly leans forward and grasps my hips, lifting me to straddle his lap. I squeak when the wine spills over my arms and down my chest, the cold liquid making me shiver. He bends down and drags his hot tongue across my skin, licking the wine from between my breasts, then along my collarbone and up to my earlobe where he nibbles lightly. I try not to react, try to keep a clear head, but instead I let out a sharp breath as my senses take a dive. Cole takes the glass from me, downing half of it while keeping those gorgeous dark eyes on mine. Then he comes in for a kiss, and that does it. I turn my head to the side; suddenly all I can picture is those lips on the blonde's. He downs the rest of the wine and sets the glass aside.

The wind picks up, blowing snow in on us. I shift down and back, and so does he, so we're both better protected from the storm, which is now becoming a blizzard. Cole pulls me back onto his lap where I meet a rather intense look. His fingers walk up my back, undoing the ties on the back of the suit. It springs forward as he lifts it over my head. My bottoms are removed just as fast, then he shifts and removes his.

He moves so his erection is between my aching thighs, with me just barely touching him, and waits, wanting me make the first move. I hesitate while I battle it out with myself, and in the end my lust wins and I slowly slide down over top of him, making us both drop our heads back, sighing. He wraps an arm around my waist and the other grips my shoulder as I start to move very slowly. I can see his muscles flexing, trying hard to give me control. His jaw is set perfectly still as my breasts bounce in front of his mouth, his stubble teasing them as they brush by. The contrast of the cold air and the hot water is an intense sensation. Cole comes in for another kiss, but I turn my face away and continue at the same pace. He growls and grits his teeth, bucking his hips to get me to move faster, but I don't. In fact, I move slower. Yes, I'm punishing him, but it's hurting me too. I hate hurting, I hate even more that he's the one who hurt me. I swallow past the growing lump, trying desperately to shove the feelings away.

"Enough of this shit." He pulls me up, flips me over the side of the tub, and thrusts back in. He lies his front over my back, holding me down. "Stop punishing me," he growls. "I only did what I had to do to get you back. I only kissed her, nothing more. I hated it, but I'd do it again if it means saving your life." He pulls out, then slams back in. "I know you're dealing with a lot, but you better let me in. If you have something to say, then say it, but don't," he slams in again, making me cry out, "ever deny me your lips, Savannah." He pounds in again, sending water spilling over the edge. He pulls out, making me whimper. "They are mine, just like this," he palms my ass, "and this," his fingers slip inside me, driving me wild. I grind my hips into him, wanting more. His other hand slips over my chest, making a point to stop over my heart. "All of it is mine, just like all of me is yours." He leans back and grasps my hips with both hands, and nudges just the tip of him inside. "Will you kiss me when I'm done fucking you?" I don't answer. I'm so pent up I'm about to jump out and roll in the snow for some kind of relief. "Savannah!"

"Yes!" I cry out as he plows back in over and over. I don't want it to end. He's the only man who has ever made me feel every possible feeling at once, but at the same time feel each individually as well. It's intoxicating. It's erotic. It's…it's…it's…I scream as every muscle clenches, sending me off toward the snowy night. He shouts and grips my shoulders, his whole body shaking on top of mine. He pulls out, flips me over, and attacks my lips. He's like a hungry animal and I'm his first meal in months. Within minutes he's entering me again, but this time he has me straddling his lap, facing him. He does all the work since I've become like jelly, but it doesn't take long for my senses to kick back in to match his rhythm.

"Cole," I moan as he bites my neck and massages my breast. "I hate that you hurt me," I confess, wanting to get it off my chest. "I hate that it was *you* who hurt me." My rocking has picked up pace; I'm close now. I'm panting, and I can feel him struggling with having to stop to talk, wanting to keep going, so I grab his face and kiss him. I'm torn too, but right now I need this closeness. I love him. This sets him off and he stands, holding me with him and sitting me on the highest seat, nearly out of the water, and hooks my legs over his shoulders. He hangs on to the side of the tub, getting in as deep as he possibly can. I clench around him, feeling full as he hits all the right places. My eyes roll up to the roof of the tent, seeing many colors dance around as I fall into a sea of passion. I couldn't be happier. Only he can make me feel this way.

"No one else," he grunts as he fills me with another hot burst of him.

We're both completely spent by the time we finish. I sit wrapped in his arms, watching the white curtain, the snowflakes dancing in a beam of light from the house. You can barely see three feet in front of us now. Cole slowly kisses my neck like he can't stop.

"Cole?" I whisper, not wanting to break this moment, but I need to, sadly. That nagging feeling is still there.

"Mmmm." His chest vibrates.

"I-ah, umm," *Fuck.*

"Tell me. It's nothing we can't handle."

*Shit, I can't. Ahhh...*I chicken out, so I go with something else that has been on my mind. "What's going to happen to my father?"

Cole sighs and holds me tighter. "It will take time, but he'll make a mistake somewhere and we'll nail him." He pauses. "Do you want your father to go to jail?"

"Yes," I say simply, because any father who can willingly hand over his daughter to someone the way he did, and kill Derek and shoot Paul...this man is not my father. He is someone else. "I'm struggling with Derek's death."

Cole turns my face around with his finger, and his look is serious. "You need to understand something, Savannah. What Derek did was wrong. That was his mistake, taking you there with no backup. It went totally against all he should have learned in his training. Whether or not he thought it was a good idea, it wasn't. That's why Derek would never have made it on the Blackstone team. He makes dangerous choices. His death is not on you." His hands cup my face so I look into his eyes. "Believe me, what happened is on him. No one blames you."

I nod in fear of saying anything. I hurt like hell on this topic. What Cole is saying makes sense. I just need time...time...I try to open my mouth and say the words to him, but I can't.

"Who hired you to come find me? I know my father didn't."

Cole cups some water, warming my shoulders. He doesn't answer right away. I know he's thinking about my question and his answer. "Sometimes when cases get as big as yours and are splashed all over the newspapers, we look into it ourselves without being asked to by the family. It didn't take us long to see there was something fishy about your case. The more we looked into it, the more things weren't adding up. So I put my men on it and we tracked you down."

"Wow," I whisper, picturing the guys chasing leads.

"When I saw your picture," he pauses, making me look up at him, "I couldn't stop staring at it. You drew me. You are so beautiful, Savannah. We pulled every string, asked every favor, sneaked in places off the grid, just to find a clue that would lead us to you. And I may have done a few things I'm ashamed of, but I don't care."

His finger hooks my chin and tilts it up, his eyes dark as night. "Baby, I'd play dirty for you any day."

I smile and give him a soft kiss under his jaw. Threading his fingers through mine, I sag back into his lap, resting his hand over my stomach. Sometimes I feel like the baby can feel him.

"I had no idea that you and I would have ended up here." He squeezes me a little tighter, then leans down, brushing his lips over the shell of my ear. "I'm sorry for what happened to you, but I'll never be sorry for tracking you down and falling in love with you."

***

"You're awfully quiet." Keith peers at me from the driver's seat. I made a lunch date with Sue today. I miss her and have only seen her once since I've been back. Keith had to go into town to pick up something from Christina's store, so he offered to drive me.

"Just thinking."

"About?"

"About...stuff."

"What kind of stuff?" he tries again.

I shake my head. Nosy bugger. "I'm just need to process some things."

"I'm a great listener." He grins. Keith has taken on the role of an older brother.

I don't want to raise any red flags with Keith since he can read me like an open book, so I go another route. "Is Dell back to replace—?

"Rent?"

"Yes, to replace Derek?" He nods, peering over at me. "I thought so."

"Dell has been waiting to work at Shadows for a long time. This will be his chance to see if he has what it takes. Plus, Logan is still looking into recruiting one of the men from the training session earlier in the month."

Something nags at the back of my brain when he mentions the recruit but quickly fades away. I can't quite bring it into focus. Keith parks the SUV in front of the UPS store, motioning for me to follow. "It's okay, I'm fine staying here," I say, smiling to reassure him.

Keith steps out and comes around to my side and opens the door. "Just because The American is in custody doesn't mean all the danger is gone." He helps me out. "Besides, I haven't put my tracking chip in you yet."

"Oh, yeah, you're funny." I follow him into the store, really not wanting to see Christina again. He holds the door open with a mischievous expression.

Shattered

"Who says I'm kidding?"

Holy hell, this place is hot! It must be a hundred and ten in here. I yank open my jacket and start to laugh. Keith eyes me funny, then gets it.

"Yeah, now you know why we leave our jackets behind." He rolls his eyes and points to the counter. "And now you'll see who Victoria's Secret's biggest fan is." Then I notice her, Christina, wearing one of the skimpiest dresses I've ever seen. She might as well be wearing a child's shirt. Wow, I don't think that could be classified as a dress. Getting a little closer, nope, that's a silk nightgown. Her hair is cut in a pin-straight bob, a different style since I saw her last. She reminds me of a pinup girl with her red lips and heavy eye makeup.

She bats her eyes at Keith but scowls when she sees me. I don't even bother to plaster a smile on my face. I'm not in the mood to play nice.

"Hello, Keith," she coos, leaning her breasts over the counter. "I believe I have a package for you and the boys. I'll go grab it." Her hips sway as she heads out back.

"Yikes," I whisper, making Keith crack up. She returns a moment later with three large boxes. I have to give her credit, I'm really not sure how she manages to walk in her stiletto heels. She looks positively ridiculous, especially considering we are in the back mountains of Montana, and in a UPS shop at that.

"Tell me, Keith, I thought Cole was coming by today." *And there it is*. "Not that I don't like seeing your handsome face." She eyes me up. "I just need to speak with him." Her freakishly red lips mold into a pout. Keith lifts the boxes and nods toward me, indicating the door, but I don't move.

"He's busy," I answer, staring at her, "but I'll let him know you said hello."

She turns, crossing her arms and pumping up her fake breasts. "Actually, if you could tell him to stop by, that would be better."

"Or I could relay the message to him," I counter, trying to control my claws that are itching to pop those fake tits.

Her smile grows just a little as she reaches under the counter and pulls out an envelope. "Oh, okay, well, be a doll and give him this. I didn't get a chance to when we were out at dinner the other night."

I don't move. I stay completely still. I've mastered this reaction as I've been blindsided enough times. Taking a step forward and reaching for the white envelope, I avoid touching her devil-red nails.

"Tell him thanks," she bats her eyelashes at me, "and I'll return his shirt to him just as soon as it gets back from the dry cleaners."

"Claressia, right?" Hot anger is starting to surface and I fight like hell to bury it.

"Saaavi...?" Keith calls out in a warning. "We're going to be late."

My nails are digging into my palms as I turn and walk out. Taking a deep calming breath of cool air helps to ground me. I slip into auto pilot and hop in the SUV. Keith is watching my face as he turns over the engine, adjusting the hot air to blast at me, but I turn it off, not wanting to thaw the icy barrier

Shattered

I'm building.

"You know it's nothing. Christina is a bitch, she's just—"

"Sue is waiting," I remind him, fastening my seatbelt. He shuts up, thankfully, and we head down the icy road to Zack's restaurant.

Brown is the color of the dirt. Ivory is like an elephant tusk. Taupe is the color of the stone in my ring. Cream is like the color of the seats, hunter green like the guys' army camo. "B-I-T-C-H!" I say in my head. It's something Dr. Roberts told me to do when I get upset. Take the word that best fits the scenario, break it down into something else and make it a better word. Let me tell you, it's *not* working.

Sue greets me with a massive hug, even granting me a kiss on the cheek. God, I love this woman; she's so warm and loving. Sometimes I swear I see a little bit of my mother in her.

"Are you sleeping all right?" she asks, mistaking my hurt for lack of sleep. I nod and slip into the seat across from her and pluck up the menu. This is a big red flag for her that something is up with me, considering we've never ordered off the menu once since coming to Zack's. He always insists we try the meal of the day, and we always do.

She waits until Keith gets settled at the bar before she turns her attention fully on me. Zack greets us with a glass of Pinot Grigio and informs us that they have Dijon salmon already in the skillet for us.

"Okay, spill it, Savi." Sue stares me down, daring me to lie. I don't, I can't, not about this. I need her help.

"Under one condition."

"What's that?" She leans closer as I begin to let her inside my head and the madness that's been eating me up inside, desperately needing release.

***

Cole

Cole pulls into Camp Green Water, where team Blackstone spent two weeks volunteering their services, and also where he is scouting out a new recruit for the house. He makes his way over to the third big warehouse where the recruits are back for more training. These are the men who made the first cut. His boots squeak across the tile floor as he nods to the captain who's blowing a whistle for the men to walk on the bottom of the pool with a brick in their hands. He blows it once, and the men drop to the bottom. Two staff sergeants are in the water with masks, ready to help if need be, and two follow up on top for a bird's eye view.

"Colonel Logan." Captain Miles shakes his hand. "So you're here to take one of my men, are you?"

Cole smirks, knowing every man would love a chance to come play at Shadows. Their reputation excites anyone who's a thrill junkie…so, most men. "I have a few in mind, but I only need one."

Miles watches as the men resurface at the opposite end. He blows the whistle again, getting them to return the same way they left. "I have three more rounds, then they're all yours."

Shattered

"Sounds good." Cole observes, keeping a close eye on the number that interests him, but then his attention is tugged to a different recruit. He moves down to the edge of the pool and watches the situation. One of the staff sergeants begins to makes a move, but Cole holds up a hand, wanting to see what will happen.

One of the men has stopped to help his teammate who got caught up in his rope. They're both struggling, needing air, but this recruit isn't giving up. He even goes so far as to pull his buddy along with him as they finish the drill. By the time they finish, the recruit is barely coherent, and his buddy is passed out but comes to quickly.

Cole takes note of his number and smiles. Savannah will be happy.

"Number nine," Cole calls out once the man is standing upright. "A word, please."

The man is wide-eyed as he takes in Cole's presence. "Colonel," he huffs, out of breath.

"Corporal Davie, nice work down there."

"Thank you, sir."

Cole rubs his face. He wasn't expecting this turn of events. "I was under the impression you had an issue with water, but what I just witnessed makes me think you've gotten over your fear."

Davie takes a long breath, looking back at his buddy. "Well, sir, you never leave a man behind. If he didn't finish, then we all don't finish." He laughs a little. "I'll be frank, I have no desire to do that again, but I will if I have to." He turns and looks at his buddy. "Pipes is a good swimmer, sir, he just got disoriented."

Cole nods, liking his answer. He couldn't have asked for a better one. "Get dried off, pick up your things, and meet me in the main office in thirty."

"Ah-yes, sir." He looks confused but does as he's told.

Exactly thirty minutes later, Davie takes a seat, dropping his bag at his feet. He looks around the office, apparently taking in the severe lack of décor in the old warehouse. Cole closes the file and glances at his cell phone, waiting for an update from Keith. He and Savi should be back at the house by now, but he knows he doesn't have time to call.

"Davie, I have to be honest. I had another recruit in mind for a position at Shadows, but after what I just saw, I think I may have to change my mind."

"Oh?" Davie can't hide his interest. He rubs his blond crew cut like he's used to it being a little longer.

"Would you be interested in a spot at Shadows?"

"Yes, I would, very much so."

Cole leans over the desk, putting emphasis on his next words to make sure he is very clear. "You understand what you will be giving up by joining the house? Relationships are next to impossible, secrets are your life, twelve to fourteen hour shifts are not unusual, and in rough elements. The house and team will become your family. I treat my men well. I haven't had a complaint yet."

Davie sits up a little straighter. "I understand, sir. I've always been interested in Shadows. I know what I will be sacrificing, but I don't have much to lose. My only family was my father, and he just passed two months ago. I have no ties. I'm basically

Shattered

a shadow already."

Cole knows about Davie's father and how he drowned off their fishing boat, but never once does Davie bring it up or use it as an excuse, and that's a damn good quality in a man. He's tough and can control his emotions. Davie is clearly a perfect match for Shadows.

"Pack your bags, Davie, we leave in an hour."

The smile that appears on Davie's face is enough to lighten anyone's mood. He grabs his bag and jumps up, holding out his hand for a shake. "Thank you, Colonel, I won't let you down."

"I know you won't."

Davie leaves just as Roth, number fifty-nine, is about to knock on the door. Cole tells him to take a seat as he opens his file and looks over the paperwork. Cole knows he is a true candidate across the board. He is the one Cole has had his eye on from day one. Roth is made for Shadows, but there is still something that niggles at Cole. "Roth, I'm sure you got wind that I've been looking to recruit a man for my house."

"I have." He leans back in his chair, looking pretty confident, which irks Cole a little. York was cocky.

"But there has to be trust." Cole watches as tiny beads of sweat break out across his upper lip. "Do you feel you are trustworthy?"

"I-I do," he stumbles. "You've seen my chart. I've passed everything with flying colors. I haven't failed one test you've thrown at me."

"I'm not questioning your physical strength or your ability. That we know. I'm talking about trust.

If there's no trust, then there's no team. No team means there's no job."

"You *can* trust me." The words come out, leaving Cole uneasy. Something feels off. He's been around long enough to go with his gut, and right now it's screaming at him to cut Roth loose.

"Then why did you swim by Corporal Davie, while he helped Pipes finish the drill? He's not nearly the swimmer you are."

He leans back in his seat and crosses his arms. "You get don't stats like that," he points to his file, "picking up the weak."

Cole clamps down on his tongue, thanking his gut and letting a few quiet seconds go by as he studies Roth's face. "Well, thanks for being honest, Roth. Now it's my turn. I don't think you're the right fit for Shadows." Roth's face falls; clearly this is not what he is expecting.

"Colonel, can you give me a chance? I'll do anything, just let me come to the house and I'll prove it." Roth looks almost panicky. Cole runs Roth's words over in his head.

"I'm sorry, Roth, but I'm staying firm on my decision. Now," Cole stands and collects his things, "I have to go. Take care, Roth. You're a good soldier. You'll do well."

Davie is standing by the front door, bags packed, with an excited grin on his face. A few of his buddies are congratulating him. When he sees Cole, he stands a little straighter and holds the door for him. Respectful, oh yeah, Cole knows he has made the right decision.

They drive directly to Zack's, unable to take him

to the house until all the documents have been signed. Frank has to go over the contracts, have Davie sign the NDA, and be sure he fully understands what is expected of him. Davie is clearly book smart and asks all the right questions. The longer Cole spends time with him, the more he feels good about his choice.

"Can I get you anything else?" The host, Adam comes over holding a pitcher of water and refilling their glasses.

"No, thanks." Frank covers his glass with his hand, indicating he doesn't want any more. "Just let Zack know we're leaving, please."

"Sure, he should be done with Nicole's paperwork by now."

Cole's head snaps up at the use of Savannah's cover name. "What?"

Adam nods and picks up a plate, balancing it in his hand. "Yeah, he spent a good hour with her earlier this afternoon. I'm not sure why, but you know Zack. He's like a vault. Anyway, she and your mother left about two hours ago, saying they needed to meet someone." A smile breaks along his lips. "So pretty and sweet with just the right mixture of sexy...man, what a combo." He whistles as he leaves the table, missing Cole's death look.

"I hope he was talking about Nicole." Frank snorts, making Davie crack up. Even Cole smiles, but only for a moment. He is confused. *What the hell is going on*?

Chapter Thirteen

Savannah

I check the clock. It's a little after six when we arrive back at the house. Sue has decided to join us for dinner. I know why, and I appreciate it. Daniel greets us as we enter the foyer. His arm still looks sore, but he refuses to use the sling. *Men.* He gives Sue a kiss and wraps me in a typical Logan bear hug while asking us how our day went. Sue speaks to him as I slip out of my coat and boots and head upstairs to change into a dress. I got wind from Abigail we are having some company when she suggested I choose something from the left-hand side of the closet. I change into a little black dress, thinking it's a safe bet, as it matches my dark eyes. I have to smile at myself in the mirror as I realize I resemble my mother more than my father. Feeling more than a little pleased and with a quick touch-up in the makeup department, I head downstairs.

"Well, well, well, if it isn't my soon-to-be wife," Dell jokes, giving me a playful smile and a small hug. "Don't you look lovely?"

"So do you, Dell. I heard you were back, glad to see it's true." I spot Cole across the room talking to Frank and someone else, his back is to me.

"Can I get you something to drink?" He wiggles his eyebrows. "Tale of the Devil?"

I laugh and hit his arm. "No, thanks! Two of those had Mark carrying me to bed last time."

"It was kinda fun," Mark jokes, wrapping an arm around my shoulder. "You were an open book of info that evening."

"Mmmmm." I roll my eyes, remembering how drunk I was.

"Can I steal you for a moment?" Mark asks, excusing us from Dell.

Mark keeps his arm around my shoulders as he walks me over to Cole. "What did you and Sue do today, Savannah?"

I look up at him, trying to see if he knows. Keith promised to keep quiet, and Keith keeps his promises. "Why?" is all I manage to get out before he interrupts.

"Melanie told me you stopped by, and you had some questions." Shit, I forgot to tell her to keep it to herself. "Are you really looking for a job in town?" Oh, he thinks I'm looking for a job. Okay, I'll let him run with that, until I speak with Cole.

"Something like that," I mutter because I hate lying.

Cole studies my face as I come up to his side.

"There she is." Frank nods. "Savannah, please meet—"

"Corporal Davie!" I reach out to shake his hand,

smiling and pleasantly surprised. "How are you?"

Frank looks at both of us, confused. "I wasn't aware you two knew one another."

Davie shakes my hand. "We met when Savannah came to the camp a few weeks back. It's nice to see you again."

Keith appears as I tell Davie it's good to see him again, giving me a nod toward Cole, wondering if I spoke with him yet. I quickly shake my head no.

"Good, Keith, you're here." Cole grins. "I wanted to ask you, would you be interested in joining Blackstone?"

Keith face lights up before he tucks it behind his mask.

"I'd be honored."

"Happy to hear that. You'll be active as soon as Savannah's," he pauses and lowers his voice, "case gets cleared up."

I roll my eyes, hating all this.

"Wouldn't want it any other way." Keith glances over at me. "You're up, buttercup."

Pressing my lips together, I shake my head.

"Could you excuse us, please?" Cole leads me away from the group with his hand on my back, directing me to his office. Once inside away from the noise, he asks me if I'd like a drink.

"Yes, whatever you're having," I answer, making him stop and turn. I never ask for a brandy.

He studies me while he starts fixing our drinks, leaning against his desk while I sip my brandy a few feet away. I'm a bundle of nerves. This could go south if I'm not careful.

"Anytime you're ready," he prompts me. "I've

got all night, baby."

I sigh, taking a rather large swig of the brown liquid and feeling it burn on its descent. Sue and I discussed this at length, but I feel like I'm about to break his heart…and possibly mine.

"Now that The American is caught, Luka is dead, Lynn is in custody, my father will be soon, and the truth is finally out," I begin, "I see my life has pretty much been a messy lie. My life has been shattered, and it's time I pick up the pieces. Since coming back this time, I've been feeling all kinds of different emotions." His face tightens a little. I can tell this is going to completely blindside him. "I need to make a change." He downs his drink, setting it aside, and folds his arms, which flex like he's holding back a reaction. I close my eyes, deciding to rip the Band-Aid off. "I need to move out." Silence. My eyes flutter open to find him staring at the floor. "Cole, I need to find out who I am before I can move forward. I just need some time." He slowly nods.

"It's not completely safe yet. Your father—" He doesn't look at me.

"Is being watched by the NYPD, so if he ever heads this way, they'll let you know. I'm only moving in town, just down the street from your parents. It's a cute little place, one bedroom, a sweet little kit—"

He suddenly stiffens. "You already found a place?"

I only nod, realizing how bad this must look. "I got a job at Zack's. I have your parents nearby in case I get into trouble, and Melanie is my neighbor.

I know this is a shock, but I really need to do this, Cole. Please understand."

He shakes his head and looks anywhere but at me. "And where does this leave us?"

I want to make sure I use the right words. He needs to know I don't want to break up; I love him. I just want some separate space so I can live a little, be Savannah Miller, the girl who has a dark past but is ready to face the light on her own two feet, not have someone looking after her. This house is amazing. It's my home, but the guys are too protective. Now that the threat is pretty much gone, I'm ready to take back my life, but before I get a chance to tell him all this, he tilts my world a little more. "You know what, maybe some time apart is a good thing. I have a trip coming up, and I don't want to have to worry about you while I'm gone."

"Don't want to have to worry about me?" I repeat his words, feeling the sting. "You want to break up?" I barely whisper, feeling my entire body tingle as the blood drains to my feet. His words slice me open. I know he worries about me, but I didn't know how much he minded it.

He scoops up his glass and moves swiftly across the room, pouring himself another drink. "You seem to have everything figured out. Seems this goes hand in hand with your plan. Besides, we knew this would have to come to an end sometime. You're a city girl, I'm a country guy. It's not a movie, Savannah. This shit doesn't work out. It's not always a happy ending. You don't belong here anymore. You don't need our protection now."

I stare at his back in utter shock. I'm moving to

Shattered

Redstone! It's like fifteen or twenty minutes from here, not New York! I can't even form a thought. So instead I place my glass down on a coaster and pull out the paper from my dress pocket, feeling like it is burning my hand. "Christina asked me to give you this. She said thanks for dinner." He quickly turns as I rest the envelope against my glass. I leave before he can say another word, but I don't miss his 'deer caught in headlights' look before I go. I don't want to break up, but I'm also not going to be the woman who stands by while another woman has time with him.

The day passes in a haze, and that night at dinner the table is buzzing with news about the house's newest recruit, Davie. He and Dell seem to be hitting it off pretty well. I wait until dessert before I share my news with the house. Keith is watching me. I think he's worried about me leaving, but I'll be all right. Cole is to my left, not eating, just nursing his drink. I won't let the hurt in—yet—not until I'm behind closed doors by myself. If I show weakness now, they'll never be okay with me leaving.

I stand, feeling slightly lightheaded, and clear my throat as the hum around the table dies and all eyes fall on me.

"What's up, Savi?" Mike asks, cocking his head to the left.

I force a smile and start, "Umm, I just want to say thank you for everything you've done for me. I've been through a lot, and if it wasn't for all of you, I wouldn't have made it. But, like they say, all good things must come to an end. You caught the bad guys, and now I'm free." I try to make a joke, but instead my eyes water. "So, I got myself a little place in town, near Daniel and Sue's, so you will be officially Savannah-free shortly." It's hard to watch their faces drop and see their eyes flicking from Cole and back to me. He is staring intently at his drink.

Dell is the first to speak, breaking the painful silence. "But is it safe?"

"If she stays in Redstone, she should be fine," Daniel says softly. "We'll keep an eye on her. Zack will too."

Mark shakes his head, looking pissed off. "You don't have to go, Savannah. None of us want you to leave."

"That's very sweet, Mark," I say, feeling the pain ooze through the cracks in my armor, and this makes me angry. "But I'm a city girl, remember. I don't belong here."

"Cole," Mark pleads to him, "say something."

"He's said enough," I interrupt, just wanting to go upstairs. "Look, everyone, you are the family I never had. I'm only in town. You'll still see me all the time; you just don't have to worry about me anymore. You can go back to being the heroes and knights for some other person in the world."

Keith shakes his head at Dell, who is about to make a comment. I decide to end on a light note before I make my exit. "Just watch your back, because you never know when Agent Black will come back."

John laughs, breaking the tension at the table. Mark smiles, but I can tell he's not happy.

Shattered

***

A glance at the clock shows it's two a.m. Sleep just doesn't seem to be happening for me. My bags are packed with everything Abigail got for me when I arrived at the house, and they are already loaded in the SUV. I'm not supposed to leave until tomorrow afternoon, but I need to get out now. Cole won't speak or even look at me, and the pain is becoming too much to bear. I just want to leave now. Yes, I'm running, but this time I can't help it. Dressing quickly and making the bed, I take one last look my room, remembering the first day I arrived here. How scared I was, how lonely I felt. I didn't think I was going to make it. I remember the first time Cole touched me, kissed me, and made love to me in the shower. A small smile comes to my lips saying goodbye, because if I don't smile I'll cry, and I'm not ready to yet.

My boots seem loud as I walk down the hallway, I grab a pair of car keys out of John's jacket, but quickly tuck them back in when I see headlights light up the entryway. I step outside just as the passenger window rolls down. I know who it is; he must have been waiting. I climb in the front seat, giving Keith a guilty smile.

"I knew you'd leave in the night." He turns the heated seats up and heads for the first gate. I watch as the massive cabin that was once my safe house grows smaller in the mirror. A part of my heart wants to run back...but it wants Cole, not the house. But he doesn't want me. I force my eyes to look forward. I must move forward and not look back.

***

Cole

Cole sits on the edge of the bed, gripping the unopened letter from Christina. He knows what it says, what they always say. She wants him back, they are perfect for one another, and she can't live without him. The fact that she gave it to Savannah makes him uneasy. He doesn't trust Christina, and her behavior is becoming more aggressive. No doubt she was hoping Savannah would read the letter. She'd fed her a fake dinner story as it was. He wants to toss it in the fire and watch those memories of her burn away, but something stops him, and he decides to keep it along with all the others as evidence in case she tries to pull something later.

"Knock, knock," his mother whispers at his open door. She is wearing her night robe. "May I?"

"Sure." He watches her as she makes her way across the room and takes a seat in his leather chair next to the fire, warming her hands with a little sigh.

"Please don't be upset with me for helping Savannah find an apartment."

Cole tosses the letter on his nightstand and leans back against his headboard. "I'm not angry. I'm just hurt that she wants to leave me. We worked so hard to stay together, and the first moment she gets a chance to leave, she takes it."

"You think that's what happened?" she asks, shaking her head. "Dear, she didn't *want* to leave, she *had* to leave." Cole makes a face, not following.

"We had a long talk over lunch today. She loves you more than anything, Cole. She left because she was feeling lost within herself. She left so she could make herself stronger so both of you could work as a couple. Don't be selfish with her, Cole. She needs this time to find out who she is."

Cole closes his eyes; he's such an asshole. This is the second time he's let his emotions get the better of him, and he lashed out at her. "I thought she was breaking up with me earlier, so I did it first," he whispers, covering his face in shame. *Fuck.*

"Well, that explains it. Oh, dear, you have so much to learn about women." She whistles and leans back in the seat.

Cole swings his legs off the bed. "Explains what?"

"Why she left in the middle of the night."

"What?" he neatly shouts. "She's gone?"

His mother moves to sit next to him. "Keith took her." She places her hand on his knee, stopping him before he interrupts. "Give her a few days, Cole. Let her settle in, then go make it up to her. She's not going anywhere. Remember, we have eyes and ears all over that town. She'll be all right."

Cole stares at the fire, listening to his mother and knowing she is right, but his gut is telling him to run to her, wanting to hold her tight and keep her safe. She gently rubs his back like she used to do when he was a boy. They sit for a long time, listening to the fire pop as he slowly relaxes and lets the realization settle that Savannah needs space from the house, from the guys, from him.

"She's my everything," he finally says with a catch in his voice. "I love her, Mom."

"I know you do, son." She kisses his cheek softly. "And you'll get her back."

"Yeah, I will."

The End

Acknowledgments

A huge thank you to Corporal George Myatte and Officer Darcy Wood.

About the Author

J. L. Drake was born and raised in Nova Scotia, Canada, later moving to Southern California where she now lives with her husband and two children.

When she is not writing she loves to spend time with her family, travelling or just enjoying a night at home. One thing you might notice in her books is her love of the four seasons. Growing up on the east coast of Canada the change in the seasons is in her blood and is often mentioned in her writing.

An avid reader of James Patterson, J.L. Drake has often found herself inspired by his many stories of mystery and intrigue. She hopes you will enjoy her books as much as she has enjoyed writing them.

Novels by the Author

Broken (Book One, Broken Trilogy)

Shattered (Book Two, Broken Trilogy)

What Lurks in the Dark (Book One, Darkness Series)

Bunker 219 (Unleash the Undead, Anthology)

All In (Second Chances Anthology)

Website:
http://www.authorjldrake.com/

Facebook:
https://www.facebook.com/JLDrakeauthor

Twitter:
https://twitter.com/jodildrake_j

Goodreads
http://www.goodreads.com/author/show/8300313.J_L_Drake

Instagram:
@j.l.drake

Pinterest:
JLDrakeAuthor

TSU:
@JLDrake

Made in the USA
Middletown, DE
04 June 2019